HUNT 6

C A Shepherd

ACKNOWLEDGEMENTS

With thanks to Sal Robinson & Siân Jones

1

"Fuckinell!" Darren Petrie exclaimed, as a lurid tabloid newspaper update flashed across the screen of his iPhone. "Listen up, boys! North West Rangers' chief youth scout, Peter Byfield, arrested on suspicion of child sexual abuse…"

"What the… ?" The rest of North West Rangers' first team swarmed around 'Dazzer' as he tried to open up the breaking news tab with a finger still damp from post-training shower.

"Give it here," North West's buff Scottish centre back, James 'Tango' Mackay, commanded, snatching the cellphone from his teammate. As Petrie hastily towelled himself down, Mackay continued reading aloud:

"Within the hour, Greater Manchester Police have arrested North West Rangers' chief youth scout, Peter Byfield, in relation to a dozen historical counts of sexual abuse against U13 players in his care from 1990-2005. Byfield, 55, has vehemently denied the allegations, yet will remain in police custody pending further investigation."

"Bloody hell!" Nathan Hunt, Mackay's centre back partner and Club Captain, exclaimed, peering over Mackay's shoulder and skim reading the article.

"Backs to the wall, guys!" the team's joker winger, German international Timo Bolz, hooted. A couple of his fellow teenage teammates let out nervous laughter.

"It's not fucking funny, Bolz," Hunt growled. "We'll

have the press swarming around the place in no time, the club's name will be dragged through the mud."

Bolz shrugged. "The article says it happened fifteen odd years ago. We've only been around for three years. It has nothing to do with us."

"Don't be so fucking naïve," Hunt responded, furiously tying the laces of his trainers, almost breaking them in the process.

"You alright, mate?" Mackay asked quietly, pulling a clean hoodie over his tousled wet ginger hair. The pair had forged a strong partnership, both in defence for the newcomers to the British Premier League and the Great Britain national team. It was a partnership that had extended on a platonic level well beyond the training ground at North West.

"We could just do without this, that's all," Hunt replied testily. Rather too testily, Mackay thought. He shot his teammate a sidelong glance. Was it his imagination, or was Nathan overreacting to something that was sick and shocking, without a doubt, but unlikely to bring down a club that had only been around two full seasons, following the amalgamation and franchising of the Scottish and English Premier Leagues?

Hunt pulled his fleece on and throwing an empty can of energy fuel in the bin with a loud clang, grabbed his shower bag and left the dressing room for the sanctity of his Jeep.

♥♥♥♥♥

"I guess you heard the news?" Alessandra Esposito queried, perching with her coffee on the sofa opposite

Nathan in the living room of his swanky red brick gated mansion on the outskirts of Manchester.

Nathan grunted, flicking idly through the TV channels until he found some American football highlights - Green Bay versus 49rs, excellent.

"Do you know the guy well, this Peter Byfield?" Alessandra queried, sipping at her coffee and enunciating the youth scout's name with distaste.

"I don't want to talk about it, Ali," Hunt replied in a low tone. He kicked his trainers off, pulled his Packers baseball cap down over his eyebrows and settled back on the couch. That was Alessandra's sign to back off.

But inside Nathan was in turmoil. This was just the last thing he or the club needed. He recalled a conversation he'd had with England team-mate, Jed Bishop, when a similar scandal had erupted at London Celtic. The press had turned up in mass, hanging around outside the ground for weeks, hounding anyone with the remotest connection to the club for information about Trevor Dean and the kids he'd molested. As club captain, Nathan would be directly in the firing line of the tabloid press. With the Dean case, the press had trawled through the playing histories of the whole squad, looking for any links, however tenuous, between individual players and Dean, on a hunt for sordid details to splash across their dirty little rags.

Nathan was no extrovert. His club captaincy and vice-captaincy of the Great Britain squad was built on the respect of his peers, sheer physical presence and fearless defensive brilliance on the pitch. Like Stevie G, Hunt's hero, Nathan did his talking on the field of play, making the central defence berth his own for both club and country alongside Tango Mackay. That was not to say he did not handle the press with aplomb, too, where he had also mastered the art of the defensive close-down, batting away attacks on the integrity of himself or the team with economic responses that fulfilled his media responsibilities and no more.

What he had really enjoyed about playing at Rangers thus far had been precisely the lack of history at the club. It was a chance to start afresh, with a brand new stadium and set of fans. Media attention had focused on the state of the art facilities at Rangers, the sleek closing roof and the raised pitch. The signing of teenage Wunderkind Timo Bolz from Bayern had been a further focus of press attention, Bolz's every move circulated around social media at lightning speed, nicely deflecting the glare of the media spotlight away from himself.

Now Peter Byfield had taken the gloss off the untarnished reputation of the club with his seedy antics. Or so it appeared. The evidence seemed fairly damning. Nathan could feel his stomach churning, the chicken mayo sandwich he'd wolfed down on arriving back home sitting uncomfortably at the top of his stomach. Having briefly scanned the story for himself on the BBC news app on his phone, he recognised the middle-aged balding guy in a blue club puffer coat. He'd seen him at the training ground a few times, when the academy players came to train with the first team. Nathan sat up, feeling the bile rise up from his stomach. He wasn't assuming the best position for indigestion.

"You're clearly not in a talkative mood," Alessandra observed, as he rearranged the cushions behind him on the sofa. "I have an appointment in town. Shall I come around later?"

"No, it's ok. Come back on Wednesday. It's the gala dinner. Leon is picking us up at seven."

"Ok," Alessandra shrugged. "Suit yourself."

He's in a weird mood, she thought, as she gathered her designer handbag and cashmere coat. Nathan could be moody. She knew he had his reasons, but there was something she couldn't quite put her finger on behind the dark storm clouds on his face that Monday morning.

2

Nick Brookes, recently appointed physio for North West Rangers Youth Academy and keen runner, leant his forehead against a tree and attempted to catch his breath, extending his right leg out behind him to stretch his calf muscle. He took in a large swig of water and gradually got his breathing back under control. He'd pushed himself a little too hard, in a bid to work off the excesses of a weekend spent celebrating his kid brother's 18th back home in Leeds.

Wiping his brow on his sweatband and running his hand through his tousled blonde hair, Brooksy, as he was known to all and sundry, settled back into a gentle jog towards the Forestry Commission car park where he'd left his newly purchased VW Golf. In truth, the hard run through the woodland just twenty minutes' drive from his rented flat in the city, was more than an attempt to sweat out the toxins in his system. It was also a chance to rid his body of the nervous tension that had been building ever since training had started back for the season.

The truth was, when he'd applied to Rangers for the new physio position at the youth academy, he hadn't expected for one minute to get an interview, let alone be offered the job. He could imagine every physio in the land would want to work in these state-of-the-art facilities, even if it wasn't with the first team - yet. He knew at least three other qualified professionals who'd applied, all with considerably more experience than himself. They were all, admittedly, considerably older as well.

Brooksy was not stupid. He knew the moment he clapped eyes on the suited guy on the interview panel that he was in with a chance. The appraising glance from the olive-skinned club executive followed by a broad smile was indicative of an appreciation of more than Brooksy's physiotherapeutic skills. It was a fucking joke that there were no homosexuals in football clubs. The places were riddled with them, from the boardroom to the boot room. Brooksy recognised at least two of the youth squad from a popular gay hangout in Manchester. It was an unwritten rule that you kept your mouth well and truly shut about such matters, not even alluding to it in the sanctity of the private physio room, should fate bring him into close contact with one of the guys in question. There was only one thing worse from Brooksy's perspective than being a gay footballer in the homophobic world of football - and that was being a gay physio. The grief if that got out to the players and press didn't bear thinking about. So, eye contact was to be avoided at all costs with any player or staff member he recognised from the numerous gay bars he frequented in the Manchester area.

Brooksy's thoughts wandered to a common resting place- Nathan Hunt. Fucking hell. The guy was even hotter in the flesh than he was on TV, where Brooksy had made a habit of tracking him on playercam, like some spotty lovestruck teenager. The old gogglebox didn't do Nathan justice, though. In person, Hunt was considerably taller, standing at least 6'3, 6'4. He had broad shoulders and the sort of absurdly muscular thighs one associated with rugby backs. The dark body hair that teased out of the V of his red Rangers top spread in a thin line down his mid torso, stopping agonisingly short before the waistband of his blue shorts.

Brooksy was yet to enjoy the pleasure of witnessing Hunt totally naked. There were only so many excuses a lowly academy physio could find for entering the sanctity of the first team dressing room, either at the Prosperity Stadium or Rangers' training ground at Marchmont Park, which the youth academy shared with the first team and reserves. Brooksy wasn't too sure he was psychologically equipped to deal with the sight of Nathan Hunt in all his glory, in any case. He probably wasn't physiologically equipped either, he grinned to himself. Just the sight of Hunt in thigh hugging shorts on Pinterest's Top 10 Footballer Bulges page had given Brooksy a hard-on. The chances of him ever treating Nathan Hunt to a post training stretch and massage were unlikely, however, unless he worked his way up the career ladder at Rangers before Hunt moved on or retired. Besides, the vastly experienced Dennis Atkins headed up the physio department for the first team, and there were at least four physios between Brooksy and Dennis, all higher up the pecking order than Brooksy when it came to career progression.

No. 6 for club and country, Nathan Hunt was certainly a superstar, albeit of the dark, brooding, understated variety. Brooksy did not think he had ever seen him smile, in all these years following Hunt's career on TV, firstly for Everton and then latterly for the newly franchised North West Rangers in the British Premiership league.

There was a certain faraway look in those dark-rimmed brown eyes, Brooksy had always thought, like Hunt's mind was elsewhere. Was it sadness? Brooksy wasn't sure. But Hunt certainly looked distracted by something. Except when he was marshalling the defence for Rangers, where conversely, he appeared ferociously driven at all times. Brooksy wasn't altogether sure what Nathan had to be sad about, if it was indeed melancholy. Hunt was on over 200k a week as club captain, as well as vice-captain of the national squad, with all the additional kudos and job satisfaction that brought. In addition, he owned that swanky pad outside the city limits, just visible beyond the gated entrance and sweeping driveway. Brooksy had driven past it a few times, out of sheer curiosity.

Then there was the ultimate footballer's accessory in stunning Italian girlfriend, Alessandra Esposito, fashion designer and heiress apparent. And the bastard was hung like a fucking horse, if the team photo in the club shop was anything to go by, where Hunt sat, thunder thighs wide apart, next to Rangers' German coach, Dieter Jantzen.

Brooksy shook his head as he jogged within sight of the carpark. He had to get Hunt out of his head. It was utterly pointless. But a boy could dream, couldn't he?

♥♥♥♥♥

Nathan swore as a message from the boss appeared on his iPhone early later that Monday evening. All players are asked to come in at 8.30 sharp tomorrow morning for a media briefing. Do not be late. That meant facing rush-hour traffic into Manchester as well as a tedious talk from the Press Officer and associated suits, undoubtedly about the Byfield business. He'd get Annie, his personal assistant, to drive him in.

It had been a quiet week so far for football news, with players only just back in training after the summer break and the transfer window yielding no multimillion pound deals as yet. This meant Peter Byfield and his sordid past took centre stage, with North West's bold blue initialled logo flashing up on the news pages of BBC and Sky News, as details of historic child abuse on his part were outlined by somber-faced sports reporters.

To make matters worse, some journo had got hold of the parents of a former youth player who had tragically taken his life at the age of 26, following a battle with drugs and depression directly linked to Byfield's post-training antics. It was a sad thing, thought Nathan, that young Ricky Fenn would become far more famous posthumously than he could ever have dreamt of in an Athletic shirt.

We never thought anything of it, when Peter brought Ricky home himself. He said Ricky needed some extra defensive drilling. Nathan shook his head, as the lined faces of Mark and Sharon Fenn appeared on the screen yet again from their home in Merseyside. Sick bastard.

He picked up his phone and dialled his agent, Fabricio. Fab was the cousin of Alessandra. It was Fab Esposito who had introduced Nathan to Ali at a party in Italy in 2015, when Nathan had been on a season's loan at Roma. Naturally cautious, it had taken a few meetings for Nathan to decide Ali could play an important role in his life. The feeling was mutual and Ali became a permanent fixture within months, relocating her fashion business from Rome to the North West of England to be closer to Nathan. They didn't live in each other's pockets; it was neither of their style. But in Ali, Nathan found the partner he needed. Sexy and sophisticated, great at making conversation with others to offset his reticence, yet a great listener, too, she was precisely what he needed, almost a shield against the crazy, imbalanced world of the sporting superstar. And in turn, wearing smoldering GB defender Nathan Hunt on her arm did Alessandra's burgeoning fashion house no harm at all.

3

Brooksy got out of his midnight blue VW Golf just in time to see NH6, Nathan Hunt's black jeep, pull into the carpark of the Prosperity Stadium. Hunt's red-headed PA was driving - a wise move, Brooksy reckoned. The traffic had been hell that morning. He extracted his gym bag from the boot and slammed the hatch shut. It wouldn't do, as a newbie member of staff, to be seen gawping at Hunt.

He wasn't entirely sure why he'd been called in to the emergency media briefing that morning by the club's Chief Executive and Chief Press Officer. It was obviously going to be about the Byfield business, but Brooksy's boss and head of physio, Dennis Atkins, didn't appear to be there.

Brooksy adjusted the collar of his club polo shirt nervously, as he took a discreet seat to the side of the main staff briefing room at the Prosperity. They'd whacked the aircon up in the room, and he actually felt cold in his brushed cotton shorts and polo shirt, despite the outside heat, that Monday morning in July.

There was a clear air of tension, as the suits came in, followed by first team and academy coaches, players in tow. The younger players were giggling nervously, Brooksy observed, while the senior pros looked altogether more somber, surely aware of the implications a sex abuse case had on the reputation and smooth running of the club. He knew that some of the senior pros had kids, too, and that surely cast a wholly different light on the sad business for them. The room gradually filled up, until there must have been over a hundred seated in the auditorium. Finally, the door opened and the unmistakable duo of Nathan Hunt and defensive sidekick, Tango Mackay, entered the room, last to take their seats.

There was a murmur of shock and disgust as Director, Owen French, confirmed that Chief Youth Scout, Peter Byfield, had been arrested and charged on 24 counts of historical child sexual abuse. Whilst the matter would need to go through the courts, there was irrefutable evidence as far as the club were concerned, and Byfield had thus been fired with immediate effect. In any case, the club could not be seen to associate with a potential paedophile, given both its global reputation and its multiple youth and kids' academies.

A call was put out for any information relating to Byfield to be reported to Greater Manchester Police and a police liaison officer had even been introduced to the room to this effect. The players were also encouraged to make use of the club counsellor if anyone was affected, whether directly or indirectly, by child sexual abuse, with the caveat that any information shared that could lead to prosecution would have to be shared with the police.

It was sickening and Brooksy could see that the nervous laughter among the youth players and younger members of the first team had been replaced by genuine shock and revulsion at the manipulative tactics employed by a seasoned paedophile. As French had commented in a grave tone, you hope and pray as a Director that this never happens at your club. Well this week, it has. And we need to find a way through these awful events and somehow emerge with our reputation intact. We are a new global franchise, building a fantastic brand and I'll be damned if we let the past of one individual ruin the future of this club.

There was nodding acknowledgement of this sentiment from the Director. The suits left the room, leaving only the Chief Press Officer, Jo Lane, behind. Lane proceeded to outline strict rules for dealing with the media to the players, giving a particularly strong warning to the youth team on the perils of misguided social media postings. It was made abundantly clear that any indiscretions, however minor, would lead to a swift taxi ride out of the club. Lane left and shortly after, the youth academy staff and players trooped out. That was Brooksy's sign to leave, as Physio to the Academy players.

But he was halted in his tracks by First team coach, Dieter Jantzen's number two, Johann "Johnny" Ziegler. "Don't go, Brooksy, you're needed here."

Brooksy looked puzzled. "Where's Dennis?"

Johnny paused briefly. "Dennis won't be with us for the foreseeable future."

"Is he ill?" Brooksy enquired. Dennis had looked deathly pale yesterday, when they'd had a morning briefing at the training ground.

Johnny took Brooksy's arm and steered him over to one side. "Sick, maybe, but not ill." He looked intently at Brooksy until the horrible truth started to dawn on the younger man.

"You're not saying Dennis is involved…" his voice tailed away as the shocking reality hit him. Byfield and Dennis were about the same age. Johnny nodded gravely.

"The police took him in for questioning yesterday. He was at Athletic and Wanderers with Byfield. Apparently, he was involved in some capacity in a paedo ring with him. More than that I don't know."

Brooksy whistled. "Fucking hell!"

"Exactly. Now not a word; that's vitally important, Brooksy."

"Of course," Brooksy nodded. Then another truth began to dawn on him. "So, you need me… to work with the first team? Is that why I'm still here?"

Johnny nodded. "You're well-qualified and the boys at the Academy really rate you already, so why not? Besides, we'll never get someone experienced in at this stage. It's too late."

"But what about the youth players?" Brooksy asked, looking confused.

"We'll get someone in. But the first team can't afford to be one man down."

A nervous smile spread across Brooksy's face, which he shut down immediately on coming to his senses. "Sorry. It's just… of course it's every physio's dream to work with the first team of a Premiership club. I didn't mean to…"

Johnny smiled. "It's ok, Brooksy, I understand. And you're right, it's a fantastic opportunity. Don't blow it!"

"I won't, Mr Ziegler, trust me," Brooksy said contritely.

"It's Johnny," Johnny grinned, then left Brooksy to compose himself. Great fucking balls of fire. There is a God after all.

4

Brooksy surveyed the plush surroundings of the Prosperity Luxe ballroom, the five-star hotel complex built as part of a multi-million development around NWR's three-tiered stadium. Tonight the ballroom was hosting NWR's annual player awards, unusually held at the start of the new season instead of the tail-end of the previous, with the aim of inspiring new players to the club to emulate the achievements of their team-mates.

Each round table seating eight was festooned with redand blue balloons, the team colours. The tables were already filling up with players, players' partners and club officials. Near the front, Brooksy could see the distinguished Spanish owner of NWR, Juan-Pedro Morales, and his stunning wife, Conchita, sat alongside Chief Executive, Owen French and his partner, Lisa. Also at the front, to their right, Brooksy spotted the unmistakable ginger mop of Tango Mackay and his girlfriend, Eilidh. Tango was, of course, sat next to Nathan Hunt and his Italian partner, Alessandra and a couple of other established first teamers and WAGS.

On a table on the stage, bedecked with a red satin cloth with blue tassels and embroidered with the NWR monogram, stood an assortment of gleaming trophies and shields. Behind the table were two giant screens, presumably to beam live pictures from the stage to the back of the room. It seemed rather unnecessary to Brooksy; the room wasn't that big and it was hardly Sports Personality of the Year!

Still, you couldn't knock the ambition of the club, and

its owner, Juan-Pedro Morales, who had insisted as a condition of his purchase that the team play in the colours of his national team, 2010 World Cup Winners, Spain.

Brooksy felt relieved to have been allocated a table place next to the Academy staff. Whilst the news of his promotion to the first team physio staff was more than welcome, he felt more comfortable for now around his colleagues of the past three weeks. The lads had been really pleased for him, if a little jealous. He would miss the players and staff at the Academy, though he would still have some involvement with them until they found a replacement for him. There had been some top bants there!

"What does a guy have to do to get some service round here?" Brooksy complained, as a waitress again bypassed their table en-route to the more pressing demands of the first team players.

"Forget it, mate," Academy coach Jez Fagan replied. "I went to the bar myself."

Brooksy made a face and got to his feet, wincing as his trousers gave him a wedgie. Borrowing his mate Pete's tux had been a bad idea. Perhaps his increased wages would extend to a made to measure dinner suit. It was bad enough having to dress up like a dog's dinner in this heat, let alone feel the material chafe on his legs and groin area.

Brooksy weaved his way around the tightly-packed round tables to the bar at the side of the room. As he stood waiting his turn, he felt a firm hand on his shoulder. He turned around. It was Johnny Ziegler.

"Brooksy, let me introduce you to our First team. Now's as good a time as any."

"Can I just get a …"

But it was too late, Ziegler was already steering him towards the VIP table at the front, where Nathan Hunt and Tango Mackay were reclining at their seats, beers in hand. Probably Heineken 0.0, knowing players these days, Brooksy thought. A tee-totaller himself, he could hardly blame them.

"Nathan, Tango, meet Dennis's replacement, young Nick here."

"Blimey, you got your GCSEs yet?" Tango guffawed, standing up and leaning across the table to shake Brooksy's hand.

"Degree in Sports Physiotherapy, Sheffield Hallam, Masters in Sports Science," Brooksy replied in a measured tone, belying none of the nerves he felt inside at meeting these two icons of the modern game.

Nathan Hunt laughed. "That's put you in your place, Tango my son!" He looked up at Brooksy without rising to his feet; Brooksy felt his stomach lurch as he stared down into those dark chocolate eyes. "Welcome to the team, Nick." Hunt smiled, a rare sight.

"Thanks, er…"

"You can call me Nathan." Hunt smiled again. Nick smiled back.

"Well, I think I'd rather have young fella-me-lad massaging my groin area that Dodgy Den!" Tango laughed. "Bloody perv."

Brooksy laughed nervously, before Ziegler whisked him off to the next table to meet some more first team players. Nathan watched him from behind. Poor guy. Looked like he was going to burst out of those trousers. Probably borrowed them from his kid brother. Nathan remembered what it was like starting out.

"Where's the missus gone?" Tango asked, nodding to Alessandra's empty seat and bringing Nathan back from his temporal reverie.

"Dunno," Nathan shrugged. "Probably gone to take a business call."

Tango couldn't work out Nathan and Alessandra's relationship. They'd been together since… well, ever since Tango had known him, since Nathan and he had signed for the new franchise two years ago. He'd met Ali in Rome, hadn't he, when he had that loan spell at Roma? Tango couldn't decide which was jammier, having Alessandra Esposito as a girlfriend or playing for AS Roma in Italy's capital. Francesco Totti, Roma's legendary former captain and 2006 World Cup winner with Italy, had been a childhood idol of Mackay. If only he had a tenth of the ball-playing skills of Totti, Mackay thought to himself. He knew he was little more than a defensive bruiser, whereas Nathan could at least spray the ball around from central defence, with some stunning diagonal passes out to NWR's wingers, Timo Bolz on the left and Darren Petrie on the right.

They seemed to be able to take or leave each other - Nathan and Ali - Tango thought to himself, while Eilidh and himself could hardly put each other down. Nights like this, where he could parade his gorgeous Scottish girlfriend on his arm, were right up Tango's street. He knew he was an ugly bugger and he wasn't convinced he would have ever been able to pull Eilidh without his sporting profile and associated bank balance. But Alessandra was in a different league from the home-grown beauty of Eilidh Sweeney. Ali was sophisticated and outrageously beautiful, as only Latin women could be. Yet there was no sign of commitment between them. If he was Nathan, he'd been making sure she didn't get away. He'd be chaining her to the fucking electric gates of that mansion in Westvale. But Ali didn't even live with him, as far as Tango knew. She had a luxury penthouse in Central Manchester, close to her fashion house in King Street.

Perhaps he was waiting until retirement, Mackay reasoned to himself. After all, there was so much travelling involved in the life of a professional footballer, especially if you played for the national team, too, as they both did. It didn't leave much time for a relationship.

"Penny for them," Eilidh nudged him. Tango turned and kissed her snub nose. "Sorry. Miles away."

♥♥♥♥♥

"What's the hold up?" Brooksy asked, reinstated back at this table nearer the back of the ballroom.

"Fuck knows," Academy Wunderkind Jamie Davies replied.

"There's some technical issues with the camera crew. I know the guy on Sound," Jordan Taylor, another youth player replied.

"Why the hell is it being filmed?" Brooksy frowned. "It's just an internal thing, isn't it?"

"For NWR TV, you know, the club cable channel," Jamie informed him. "But don't worry, they'll just home in on the first team and the boss. They always do. The best us minions can expect is our twenty seconds of fame when the best Academy player award is handed out."

"Who will that be, then, *you* mate?"

"Either myself or Blakey," Jamie replied to Brooksy in all seriousness. Winston Blake was the Academy's lightning fast wingback. At 16 years 11 months, he was a good year younger than Jamie, which made his achievement of playing in a Carabao Cup match for NWR all the greater than Jamie's own debut for the first team at the end of the season, when Rangers had thrown a few squad players and Academy kids into the team for some dead rubbers, Europa league place already assured for the next season.

They were a good bunch of lads, Brooksy thought to himself. Whilst he was a good six or seven years older than most of them, he enjoyed the craic with them. They were still keen to impress and therefore carried little of the arrogance of the first team pros he had encountered thus far whilst making Dennis's room his own.

Brooksy wasn't sure what he was going to do the first time he had to give Nathan Hunt a rubdown. Good god, that guy was hot. He'd had some subtle but sexy aftershave on as well, when Brooksy had been introduced to him a little while ago. Nothing he'd come across before. Probably not available over the counter, Brooksy thought to himself. Hunt had probably bought whatever it was he was wearing online, at a thousand quid a bottle, Brooksy reckoned.

Brooksy was disturbed from his internal monologue by the maitre d' for the evening, local hero and ex-City player, Andy Marsh, his post-retirement bulk squeezedinto a tux even tighter than Brooksy's own.

A series of long monologues from various club

luminaries followed and Brooksy tried to focus on familiarising himself with the ethos of his new employers.

5

A friendly against Glasgow Rangers - dubbed the Battle of the Power Rangers by the local press - was to be Brooksy's first experience of working with the first team. The match was to be played at the Prosperity that Tuesday evening and the club had already sold a respectable thirty thousand tickets for the game.

Brooksy would sit pitch-side with senior physio, Lucia de Sousa, and the subs. Dieter Jantzen was using the game to blood a few of the new signings, including Dirk Van de Huizen snapped up from FC Twente in the summer and promising young Welsh midfielder, Huw Simons.

Young German superstar, Timo Bolz, would start on the bench, though Jantzen was sure to bring him on at some point, or there would be complaints from the 30,000 home fans and 1000 strong visiting Glasgow Rangers fans in the away section behind the goal. While Nathan Hunt might be the best-paid player at the club, Timo Bolz was certainly the highest profile at this current point in time. With his shaved back and sides and a floppy white blonde quiff of hair swept back from his eyes by a thin black band, he was the rebel boy pin-up of the team, his number 9 shirt easily outselling his closest rival, Hunt, by a good three to one ratio. Not that Nathan Hunt cared. He wore his superstar status lightly, the NH6 number plate on his understated black Jeep about the only nod to his celebrity credentials.

Through the open door of the physio room, Brooksy could see the first team players drift into the home dressing room. He felt a little shiver of anticipation as he saw Hunt and Mackay enter and take up their established positions at numbers six and five respectively. It was a shame that a wall pillar was in the way, obstructing a clear view of Nathan's berth, his red Hunt 6 shirt hanging up ready for him to change into. Short of fabricating some tenuous excuse to enter the dressing room, he wouldn't be able to see Hunt in all his glory. Brooksy returned to his notes for the evening, and checked he had the correct gear in his bag.

"Hey, heard the latest on Byfield?" Petrie yelled above the Imagine Dragons playlist.

"He's booked you in for a soapy massage, Dazzer?" Mackay cracked back. There was raucous laughter and slapping of Petrie's bare buttocks as he slipped into his blue home shorts.

"Not fucking likely," Petrie retorted. "Fucking queer pervert."

Nathan winced at the turn of phrase. Could he be bothered to challenge Petrie on it? He certainly ought to, as Club Captain and role model, even if his natural inclination was to keep his head down. It was going to be a long season if he didn't put a stop to the sort of homophobic banter that had reared its ugly head since news of Byfield's arrest had broken.

Nathan paused the music which succeeded in gaining everyone's attention.

"Less of the homophobic comments, please. Byfield's a paedophile. He may or may not be homosexual, that's got nothing to do with it."

There was a silence before Petrie muttered an apology and Nathan switched the Dragons back on.

Brooksy overhead this exchange from the sanctity of

the physio room. Hunt went up a further notch in his estimation. Not that it would make any difference, if the past few days' training field banter was anything to go by. As far as most of the players were concerned, homosexuality belonged in the same category as child sex abuse. Something you joked of and made disparaging references about, whatever your private views on the matter. It was all part of the dressing room culture in the anachronistic world of football, from elite to grassroots.

He'd read somewhere that a BBC documentary on homophobia in sport had tried to secure an interview with some Rangers players last season, but nobody had volunteered. That had shocked him a little. He had expected that the likes of Hunt, at least, would have wanted to cast the club in a good light in these politically correct times they lived in.

Homosexuality still appeared to the hot potato nobody wanted to touch, Brooksy mused. It was undoubtedly linked to the sexual abuse scandals that had emerged in recent years. Brooksy was in no doubt that there were hundreds, possibly thousands, of young men who hadn't come forward to report abuse at the hands of abusive trainers, from grassroots to professional level. It was a tragic thing, that these young men carried so much shame and self-abasement about what had happened to them, as if to admit it was tantamount to saying they enjoyed it. And nobody wanted to be labelled a homosexual in the football dressing room. Because to be gay cast a question over your motivation for playing -Brooksy knew how the warped logic worked. To be gay meant you were constantly leching after your team-mates. Woah betide you if you found yourself in the team showers with a gay boy.

Brooksy had heard all that nasty shit many a time over the years, from the short time he had played in a youth team, before rupturing his cruciate ligament, to more recently, through working with the Academy players, especially in the wake of the Byfield affair. He didn't doubt that a small percentage of footballers must be gay or bisexual. If national figures were between 5 and 10%, then he reckoned - notwithstanding the disinclination towards macho sports expressed by many gay men - that around 5% must be queer at any one time. In a squad of 30, that meant at least one player would be gay or bisexual.

Brooksy cast his eye over the team-sheet and list of substitutes in his hand. If he had to put money on it, he'd say Bolz, with his quiffy hair and skin-tight Calvin Kleins, was the most likely candidate. Vain little shit, Brooksy thought to himself. Still, he couldn't deny that Bolz was a fantastic player. The hierarchy obviously thought so, too, unanimously voting Bolz as Young Player of the Year at last night's awards, despite Bolz only signing for Rangers at the end of the January transfer window and finishing with less goals and assists than Darren Petrie on the opposite wing. Petrie, to his credit, bore him no ill will. It was blindingly obvious just what a special talent Bolz was and they all knew just how fortunate they were that Bolz had chosen Rangers over City or United.

Brooksy perched on the end of the massage table as Jantzen and Ziegler entered the dressing room to deliver their team talk. True it was just a friendly and nobody wanted to dive in with stupid tackles and risk being out for the season starting, but there was an element of grudge to this match, given some ill-judged comments Tango Mackay had made to the press on leaving Glasgow Rangers for North West two years ago. Mackay had made out North West offered him a greater challenge than the mighty Rangers of Scotland, which had not gone down well with either the Rangers management or their ferocious legions of supporters north of the border. Suffice to say, Mackay was glad this was a home friendly. There was only so much heckling a thousand odd Glasgow Rangers fans could make in NWR's huge three tier stadium.

It was a warm mid-July evening, and Brooksy enjoyed feeling the early evening sun on his back as he took his place alongside the subs, in the plush red and blue home team seats behind the gaffer and first team coach. He had been told to shadow Lucia for the spate of friendlies coming up, so that he would be up to speed for the start of the season. A couple of the eleven selected had small knocks and it would be interesting to see how they held up. Others had returned to training too out of shape to play tonight. Ziegler's punishment for the three culprits was to name and shame the trio in the club press conference a seat in the stands with the public, where they would undoubtedly face some awkward questions from NWR fans and in all probability a chorus of You Fat Bastard!

The unmistakable drum beat of Queen's *We Will Rock You* emanated from the tannoy as the two teams prepared to emerge from the tunnel and onto the pitch perfect field of play. Thirty-five thousand hands clapped in unison to the iconic track as North West Rangers in cherry red shirts, royal blue shorts and socks ran onto the pitch and dispersed to the left, while their Glaswegian opponents in their historic blue shirts, white shorts and black and red socks, ran to the right towards the away fans, applauding them for their efforts in making the two hundred mile trip to the Prosperity Stadium just north of Manchester.

Nathan puffed his chest out and took a deep breath as the team lined up for the customary handshakes. This is where he got to reacquaint himself once more with his all-time sporting hero, Rangers boss, Stevie Gerrard. He'd met him already a few times at various football awards ceremonies, where the two had exchanged a few words, neither of them being disposed to lengthy verbal exchanges!

"Alright, mate?" Stevie greeted him in that unmistakable Scouse tongue, pumping Nathan's hand.

"Not too bad at all, Stevie," Nathan replied, slapping Gerrard's forearm.

Formalities undertaken, the coin was spun in the air by Hunt, who had won the toss, and NRW elected to shoot towards the away end, giving them the second half to fire a couple into the net in front of their own fans in the Raul stand, named after the iconic Spanish forward.

The French referee blew the whistle and the match was underway. Brooksy, in his white polo shirt and navy brushed cotton club shorts, felt a surge of excitement well up inside. This was it, this was the dream. He, Nick Brookes, recently qualified physio, was sat here on the bench of a top Premiership football team, where every so often, the TV cameras would pan across its occupants. He'd taken his chances, ridden his luck, and here he was in dreamland.

He wondered if they would pass comment on his inclusion. It was, after all, big news that First Team Physio, Dennis Atkins, had been escorted out of the club alongside Peter Byfield. It was fair to say Brooksy had been in the right place at the right time, albeit under inauspicious circumstances.

Brooksy winced alongside the majority of the crowd, as Tango Mackay brought down a Rangers defender with a juddering side tackle. The Glasgow Rangers player got up manfully and after mouthing a torrent of expletives at Mackay, handed the ball over to a teammate to take the free kick. This was all the excuse the away fans needed to break out into a chorus of *Yer Club is full o' paedos* to the tune of The Referee's a Wanker.

Nathan grimaced. This was precisely the sort of crap he'd feared. It would only get worse when the season started in earnest, and those paltry one thousand travelling fans would mushroom into ten thousand plus baying away fans from the plethora of teams from the North West and Midlands who regularly played fixtures here in the British Premier League. He gestured to the home fans to rack up the noise. They duly obliged, drowning out the Scots with a rousing rendition of the song devised with humorous deference to the club's Spanish owner and ironic reference to the last minute surrendering of the British League Cup to their rivals, City: *We're off to sunny sunny Spain, Y Viva the Rangers. We're gonna win the Cup again, Y Viva the Rangers!*

Nathan needn't have worried. Timo Bolz managed to

silence the away fans in five frantic minutes, as a series of one twos with Welsh wizard, Huw Simons, led to two sublimely taken goals by the German teenager. A penalty coolly taken by NWR's number ten, Zak Lewin, and the home team were three nil up already as the referee blew for half time.

Brooksy followed the players into the dressing room. Ziegler had already told him to check out a few of the players who'd received knocks in the first half and get some of the players on the bench prepared to come on at the hour mark. Lucia would advise him if needed.

Job duly done, Brooksy dashed to the loo quickly before he was due back pitch-side. He took a sharp intake of breath as he caught sight of a familiar figure in the mirror above the hand dryer on the wall. Fucking hell, it was only Nathan Hunt stood at the urinal, and the angle of the mirror meant he could see everything in the glass reflection.

Shit, Brooksy swore under his breath as his spray went haywire. He looked down furiously, hoping Hunt hadn't heard him curse. He shook off the drops then snuck quietly out of the restroom and back onto the pitch, trying to forget what he had just seen in the mirror and focus on the task in hand.

♥♥♥♥♥

Nathan stretched his long limbs out as he finally basked in the comfort of his super king-size bed later that evening. It was great to get the first game of the new season out of the way, even if it was just a friendly. Not that any game against the multiple Scottish champions was ever a convivial affair and Nathan had the bruises to show for it. The stud marks down his right calf had finally stopped smarting, but the nagging ache of a thigh strain would need some treatment in the morning.

The new guys had fared well, Nathan thought, especially the young Welsh boy. Huw Simons hadn't looked at all out of place in a team full of seasoned internationals. He'd be knocking on the door of the GB national side in the next year or so, Nathan reckoned. They were getting younger all the time, the kids joining the senior squad at Bisham Abbey.

Nathan was feeling pretty pleased with how his body had shaped up. He wasn't one of the spring chickens anymore, and despite the GB's team ignominious early exit from the Euros, it still felt like he'd barely had a summer off between last season and this. At least Rangers had qualified automatically for the Europa League this season by token of finishing fifth in the league and wouldn't face several weeks of torturous qualifiers against Eastern European small-fry in some god-forsaken corner of the continent.

Nathan reckoned they were in a pretty good place, on the whole, managing to retain their top players and acquire the services of teenage superstar, Bolz, as well. Some of the chavvy English kids from the Academy that had irritated the hell out of Nathan last season had been replaced by more experienced foreign imports. While that wasn't good news for the progression of home-grown talent, Nathan much preferred a few taciturn but technically astute lads from overseas over the teenage bling brigade any day, with their endless run-ins with the coaching staff and godawful choice in rap music. Yes,

Rangers should definitely be pushing for a Champions League spot this season, alongside some of their more illustrious rivals from the North West, and if the draw worked out well for them, they could easily make it to the Europa League final this time, in Nathan's view, so long as they could avoid either of the Milan teams in the knockout stages.

His phone beeped and Nathan reached over to his bedside table. It was his agent, Annie, with his diary for the following day. The boss had kindly given them a later start after their first run out, so there would be some light training late morning and that was all. Nathan would see how his thigh was holding up in the morning; it might be more prudent to get some physio instead. Then it was a trip to Manchester Children's Hospital with a couple of the lads for some promotional work on behalf of the NWR Community Trust. Nathan didn't mind these gigs; he had little time for idiots and attention seekers but all the time in the world for sick kids and those who couldn't help themselves. Besides, it was nice to reconnect with real life every so often. In Nathan's view, the young players coming through now were little more than narcissistic slaves to consumer culture and social media, with the emotional intelligence of the average primary school kid. It was rare to find anyone under the age of 25 with any sort of maturity or nous about them.

Nathan removed his t-shirt and turned the lamp off. Time to sleep. He was glad the season was soon upon them. Unlike most of the senior pros, he enjoyed the sensation of physical exhaustion in his limbs from the first few weeks of training. It was a healthy tiredness, helping him sleep uninterrupted, minus the nagging anxieties that circled like birds of prey in his head during the off season, disrupting his sense of equilibrium and rendering him moody and crochety by day. Nathan was a person who needed routine to keep the demons at bay.

6

What the f.... Brooksy exhaled, as he approached the Rangers training complex at 9.30am the next morning. He slowed down to a halt as, instead of hanging an easy left into the carpark, he was forced to join a queue of players and staff in their cars of assorted sizes and specs, backing up on the entry road to Marchmont.

Something was occurring, that was for sure. He could see a number of policemen and women in fluorescent vests, speaking into their radios at the entrance, with half a dozen or so squad cars parked haphazardly in the carpark. Several vans were stationed in the slip road, beyond the turning into the carpark, with satellite disks on top - TV crews by the looks of it.

Brooksy got out of his car and approached the black Audi in front of him. It was one of the youth players Brooksy knew from the Academy.

"What's going on, Panko?"

"Not a Scooby," Stevie Pankhurst shrugged. "Just got here myself and my phone's out of juice.." He nodded towards the vans beyond the carpark. "SkyNews are here, though. Must be something big. Reckon it's to do with the paedo physio…. Sorry, mate."

Brooksy grunted at Pankhurst and returned to his car to await further instruction. He flicked over from the rock station to Radio 5, with its constant stream of news, particularly of the sporting variety. He didn't have long to wait.

Now for the latest from Marchmont, North West Rangers' training ground, where it is understood the body of a youth player has been discovered by staff opening up this morning. We cannot yet confirm the name of the player until his family have been informed but we understand there are no suspicious circumstances involved.

Brooksy felt sick. A suicide by the sounds of it. His phone sprung to life, with a flurry of social media notifications. He clicked immediately on a message from Johnny Ziegler. *There will be no training today, owing to the tragic event at the club. Please go home and await further instructions.*

Fucking hell.... Brooksy joined the queue of vehicles waiting to perform a U-turn beyond the carpark entrance and caught his breath. First the Byfield affair, and now this... what the hell was going on?

♥♥♥♥♥

Nathan had been summoned to the gaffer's house for an emergency club meeting with the Chief Executive and Chief Press Officer, as well as Jantzen, Ziegler and the Head of the Youth Academy, Aaron Willows. It had been decided to avoid the Prosperity Stadium, where the TV crews were also stationed, anxious for the whiff of the slightest bit of activity. The club flag had been lowered over the stadium, which was the only morsel of information available for them to report on, beyond the limited police statement issued earlier that morning.

"Nathan," Jantzen noted soberly, opening his own front door to the Rangers' captain. Nathan simply nodded and followed him into the minimalist living room he'd visited on a couple of occasions before.

He poured himself a black coffee from the pot on the table and took a seat next to Johnny Ziegler. On the wall, the gigantic 60 inch television was tuned to News 24, where a female reporter in a sleeveless blouse stood somberly outside the Prosperity Stadium, pontificating with the news anchor in the studio what might have happened at Marchmont. A few moments later, it flicked to a male reporter outside the training complex, which was now a sea of white and yellow police cars and vans.

"Do we know anything else?" Nathan asked Ziegler. Ziegler nodded and handed Nathan his iphone.

"Oh fuck," Nathan swore, reading a long text from Matty Lorca, the youth academy kitman. It turned out that Matty had gone to the training facility just before 8.30 that morning to sort some kit for an academy match that evening. He'd gone into the changing rooms to check for stray kit when he'd found a club holdall and Rangers kit on the floor. Puzzled, he wandered into the shower rooms, which is where he stumbled upon the tragic truth. Carey Hopkins, a 16 year old academy player, was lying foetal on the wet room floor, face deathly white, already coagulated blood covering his wrists and pooled on the floor around his skinny, white, dead body. He'd slashed his wrists and bled to death.

"But what was he doing there alone?" Nathan asked, once the initial shock had subsided. He looked up. Dieter Jantzen was simply staring out of the dual aspect panoramic window in the living room. The Chief Marketing Executive was on the phone, while the Chief Executive had his head in his hands. It was mind-numbingly grim. The poor kid… and the poor lads who were his teammates, they would never be the same. And as for the parents… it didn't bear thinking about. Nathan felt sick.

"We think he hid there overnight. The club doctor told Matty that the kid had only been dead a few hours when Matty found him. Looks like he took his own life this morning, having spent the night there. Did you know him?"

Nathan shook his head, peering at the photos of a young freckled ginger lad on Ziegler's phone. "Must be a recent addition. I've never seen him in my life before. But I don't have much to do with the Academy kids. Was he any good?" Nathan winced. "Sorry, that sounded crass."

Ziegler shrugged. "Pretty nifty on the wing, apparently. Needed bulking up, like lots of the younger ones."

Well, he won't be bulking up now, Nathan thought grimly. He got up, feeling his stomach cramp. He walked over to the window and stood a few feet apart from Jantzen. Outside the sky was cloudless, the sun toasting the treetops visible in the distant from the elevated position of Jantzen's house on the hilltops.

"This is truly terrible, Nathan," Jantzen muttered. "First Byfield and Atkins, and now this."

"Do you think there's any link?" Nathan asked. The press were already asking the self-same question.

Jantzen shrugged. "I can't see how. The sex abuse cases were historical and neither Byfield nor Atkins worked at the Academy. This looks like a mill run teenage suicide."

Nathan forgave him the malapropism in the circumstances. "When are the club going to release the identity?"

"They're trying to get hold of his parents. They're still on holiday in Portugal. The kid was staying with his cousin while they're away."

"Holy shit," Nathan swore. "Poor sods."

"How's the thigh this morning?" Jantzen asked, somewhat incongruously.

"Bit tight, Could do with some physio. Think I might still have one of Fernando Fucking Ruiz's studs in my calf, too."

"That guy's an animal," Jantzen muttered. "Stevie G needs to give him a talking to." Nathan concurred. It provided a brief moment of respite from the shocking news.

♥♥♥♥♥

Like the vast majority of Rangers staff, Brooksy was glued to the television screen, mobile in hand, alternating between titbits of inside knowledge and expressions of shock from all those associated with the club, and News 24.

It had not been a good morning so far, it would be fair to say. Not only had Brooksy been forced to make a U-turn and return to his rental pad in Central Manchester, he'd also bumped into his ex, Harv, who'd made the journey across from Sheffield to pick up the last of his gear, following their less than amicable split a month ago. Harv, a jobbing actor, had made the trip up north with Brooksy, following his successful interview at North West Rangers, but had found work harder to come by, despite Brooksy's assurances that Manchester was buzzing for the arts and Ali would find no problem finding suitable employment. In truth, Harv had not expected Brooksy to get the position at North West and had made the promise to relocate on the assumption it would not come to fruition.

"You could have let me know first," Brooksy commented, as Harv appeared in the living room with a full holdall.

Harv shrugged his wiry shoulders. "I assumed you wouldn't be in. You're not normally, this time of day."

"Come here often without me knowing, then?" Brooksy queried archly, eyes not leaving the television set.

"No. This is the first time," Harv lied, having used the apartment on several occasions for casual sex in the daytime.

"Well you can leave the key, this time. I won't be seeing you again."

Harv paused. "Sure." He took it off his keyring and flung it across the table, banging the front door shut behind him.

"Thank fuck for that," Brooksy muttered to himself, then sat up as a slightly fuzzy picture of a ginger headed lad filled the TV screen.

The body found at Marchmont, North West Rangers' training ground, this morning, has been identified as that of Carey Hopkins, aged 16, a member of the Rangers Youth Academy. His family, who are on holiday in Portugal at the moment, have been informed. There are no suspicious circumstances around the death of Hopkins, a promising young winger for the Youth Team. Police have requested that the family and friends be left to grieve privately at this immensely difficult time.

Suicide, obviously, Brooksy grimaced. This was truly terrible. What on earth had driven a young lad with his whole future ahead of him to take his own life? He must have been pretty good to be part of the Rangers Youth set-up and even if he'd failed to secure a senior contract with the club, he'd more than likely be taken on elsewhere at a professional club, with NWR on his CV. Brooksy recognised the lad from the photo, though in truth, he'd barely got to know the young players before he'd been whisked off to work with the senior squad. Hopkins was a local lad, as he remembered, with a strong Mancunian accent and a freckled baby face. He could imagine Hopkins being subjected to some macho mickey-taking from some of the more physically mature lads in the squad, but nothing more than that. In Brooksy's experience, kids today were altogether kinder and more tolerant that their forefathers, certainly if some of the backroom tales Dennis had told him were true, in the brief time they had worked together.

The TV screen panned aware from the shots of police milling around Marchmont and back to the blonde reporter outside the Prosperity Stadium. The gates were being opened by a staff official to allow several expensive cars drive in, undoubtedly Senior Management and the boss.

We are hearing now that the Chief Executive of North West Rangers, Owen French, has called a press conference for midday. Of course, the BBC will be staying here to bring you these pictures live here. To recap...

Brooksy watched, as several suits emerged from the first car, followed by Dieter Jantzen and Club Captain, Nathan Hunt. Hunt looked bronzed and muscular in a white club polo-shirt and royal blue tracksuit bottoms.

Within half an hour, Chief Executive Owen French was sat behind a table draped in the blue and red club colours, flanked by a somber Nathan Hunt to his left and an emotional Dieter Jantzen to his right. Before a packed press room at the Prosperity Stadium, French confirmed the terrible news that Carey Hopkins, a promising young player from the Rangers Youth Academy, had tragically taken his own life earlier that morning. He made the usual appeal for privacy to allow the grieving family to come to terms with their loss, whilst also highlighting the vulnerability of young team-mates who would undoubtedly be traumatised by both the loss of their teammate and the circumstances in which it had happened. Trained counsellors and experienced club officials were already working with the lads, at a venue separate from the cordoned off training complex where the tragic events had unfolded.

Jantzen expressed the shock of all at the club at this terrible loss and passed on the condolences of the Senior team to the family and friends of Hopkins, while it was left to Hunt to promise that Rangers would be doing their utmost this season to bring back a cup and hopefully a Champions League spot in honour of Carey.

French batted away the anticipated insensitive questions around the method of suicide and the three left the room.

Brooksy flicked the TV off. Enough was enough.

He didn't need to play black tv tourist anymore. He got changed into his running gear and grabbed his car keys.

♥♥♥♥♥

Brooksy immediately felt the gloom lift as he plunged into the cool green woodland of Lime Forest, a welcome tonic from the humid urban streets around his city centre pad, where the pavements were literally steaming from the heat. He felt the satisfying crunch of dried twigs under his feet as he pounded down the gentle incline towards the lake at a steady pace. Whilst he was reaping the benefits of the state of the art facilities at North West's gym, nothing could beat the feeling of being out in nature, away from the noise and stress of the increasingly insane "reality" of modern life, the musky pine smell of the firs and other greenery imbuing his olfactory senses as he slalomed between the trees. It was the only place where Brooksy could truly switch off from what he knew to be the fleeting yet unavoidable stresses of everyday life and regain perspective.

"What the fu...!" Brooksy hissed as he was sent sprawling to the ground by a sudden force. He rolled over onto his back, shielding his eyes with his hand from the sun piercing through the trees as he tried to assess the situation. He was immediately covered in slobber by a gleeful brown boxer dog. Brooksy heard adult feet pounding in his direction.

"Fury, off!" a deep, male voice commanded. The dog paid no attention and carried on his affectionate greeting. Suddenly "Fury" was yanked off and Brooksy heard the click of a lead behind attached.

"Y'alright, mate?" a vaguely familiar voice enquired, extending a hand to pull Brooksy to his feet.

Brooksy squinted as he stood vertical once more. It was Nathan Hunt, his face a picture of friendly concern. Brooksy groaned inwardly. Of all the people to fall arse over tit in front of, even if it wasn't exactly his fault.

"Sorry about that. Fury's still in training," Nathan apologised, but his brown eyes gave away his amusement.

"Clearly," Brooksy replied shortly, brushing the dried leaves and debris off his running vest and straightening his shorts.

"Aren't you the new physio guy?" Nathan enquired, frowning as he racked his brains for a name.

"Yeah. Nick Brookes - Brooksy," Brooksy replied. "Sorry, don't recall your name."

Nathan looked taken aback then realised Brooksy was taking the piss, despite his obvious annoyance at being bundled over by an over-enthusiastic Fury.

"Getting away from it all?" Nathan enquired. Brooksy nodded. "Terrible news."

"Yeah," Nathan concurred. There was an awkward pause. "Do you come here often?"

They both laughed at the cliché.

"Once or twice a week, gets me out of town. Gym facilities are amazing, but…"

"They don't sort your head out," Nathan added, reading his mind. Brooksy nodded. There was another awkward pause.

"You've not got your running gear on, though," Brooksy observed.

Nathan shook his head. "I've got a slight thigh strain from the Rangers match. Was going to come in and get some physio today, actually, but…"

"Yeah," Brooksy nodded. "Think we'll be open as usual tomorrow?"

Nathan shrugged. "It depends if Marchmont's still a crime scene. I reckon they will have done all their forensic stuff by then. But it's whether we want the kids to use the same showers and changing room etc."

Brooksy nodded slowly. "Of course."

"So, I expect we'll be training at the stadium at least, not sure what they'll do about the youth."

There was a pause. "Well, it was nice bumping into you, Brooksy," Nathan grinned, Fury's lead wrapped tightly around his wrist so that Fury was straining against it in vain.

"Didn't really have a fucking choice, did I?" Brooksy commented, taking a swig of water.

"Might see you tomorrow, then, for physio?" Nathan enquired.

"Depends who's on." Brooksy shrugged nonchalantly, belying the thumping of his heart inside his ribcage. "Maybe."

He broke into a gentle jog and left Nathan and Fury behind in the clearing.

"Cocky little shit," Nathan commented to the dog, watching Brooksy's toned figure disappear through the trees.

7

Nathan swore under his breath as he was forced to slow down a few hundred yards before the electronic gates leading into the Prosperity Stadium. A couple of hundred journalists and photographers were gathered outside, dictaphones and cameras at the ready, eager for the paltriest of scraps to feed the local and national press concerning the tragic death of Carey Hopkins. Refusing to wind his window down, Nathan honked the horn of his Land Rover and flashed his lights, making it clear he was not playing ball. He resisted the temptation to shout some choice expletives as the frustrated journos banged on the side of the car as he crawled through the slowly opening doors. They knew better than to trespass inside the ground, where a line of security guards had been drafted in to deal with the inevitable publicity this event would generate.

"Fuckin nightmare," Nathan grunted, parking up next to Tango's red Lambo outside the players' entrance. It clashed horrendously with the defender's hair.

"Least we get to train behind closed doors, eh," Tango replied, swinging his sports bag over his shoulder and walking alongside Nathan towards the doorway into the back of the stadium.

"There's that," Nathan conceded. Undoubtedly Marchmont would have been a bearpit, were it open for business today. It was no longer a crime scene, but out of respect for the family of Carey Hopkins, it had remained shut for the time being.

"What have they done with the kids today?" Tango enquired, as they entered the home changing room.

"They've got the day off," Nathan replied. "I heard the police are paying home visits to some of the lads in the youth team."

"Poor sods," Tango commiserated, changing into his training kit. "As if suicide of a team-mate's no bad enough withoot 101 questions from the polis."

Nathan loved the way his Scottish teammate pronounced police *polis*.

The head physio came in. "Nathan - you need to get that thigh looking at before you train. Timo, I want that ankle checking out, just to be double sure. The rest of you, outside."

The familiar clattering of studs echoed out from the home changing room to the tunnel. Nathan headed towards the physio rooms.

"You're with Brooksy today, mate," the head physio informed him. "Linda's with the boy wonder here.

"Downgraded in her affections, am I?" Nathan grinned, swiping Timo Bolz's carefully coiffed blonde thatch as the young German pushed past him into the head physio's suite.

Nathan took a left into the adjoining room, where he recognised the fair-haired Nick Brookes.

"Recovered from yesterday?" Nathan enquired, grinning, as he perched on the end of the table.

"Yeah, I didn't push myself too hard, it was pretty humid," Brooksy replied, back to Nathan as he washed his hands.

"I meant the mauling from Fury."

"It was nothing," Brooksy shrugged. "Just took me by surprise, that's all. Thigh a bit tight, isn't it?"

"Yeah, left thigh," Nathan replied, lying on his back.

He took a sudden intake of breath as Brooksy's hands felt cold on his inner thigh. He winced slightly as Brooksy pressed his thumbs into his thigh muscle.

"That hurt?"

"It's just a bit sore. I felt it when I booted a ball out of defence in the game against Rangers. Don't think it's anything too serious."

"Scuse me," Brooksy muttered, pushing Nathan's shorts up on one side to carry on his examination.

Fuck! Nathan cursed inwards, feeling his cock twitch as Brooksy's hands brushed against his scrotum.

"Just bring your knee up, will you," Brooksy commanded, "just going to give your thigh a rub down."

It was at that point that Nathan's stiffening cock, mercifully still encased in his white briefs, decided to edge out of the side of his shorts. Christ almighty, no, Nathan groaned inwardly. Brooksy turned away tactfully to get some Deep Heat. Feeling his own manhood rise to the occasion, he hastily pulled his polo shirt out of his shorts, hoping to God Nathan would not notice his sudden sartorial inelegance.

By the time he had acquired the necessary equipment, Nathan had stuffed his errant manhood back inside his shorts and pulled his own shirt out over his boner. Had Brooksy noticed, Nathan wondered. What a fucking nightmare. He'd heard all sorts of stories about guys getting hard-ons at the wrong moment, usually during moments of heightened emotion, like singing the national anthem at Wembley, or when the spine-tingling Champions League music blared out the speakers, or even during goal celebrations. But not alone in the fucking physio room with another guy like this.

Nathan was so intent on avoiding Brooksy's eyes at all costs, that he entirely missed the tell-tale bulge in the younger man's brushed cotton shorts.

"That's you done, mate. You can join the others. I don't see there being a problem. Come back and see me if there is - or Luisa," Brooksy added hastily, also avoiding the other man's gaze, though not entirely for the same reasons.

Fuck fuck fuck! Brooksy exhaled, once Nathan had left. He shut the door and leant back against it. He looked down at himself, his boner still evident beneath his polo-shirt, a thousand and one thoughts passing through his head. Finally, he broke into a smile. The club photo he'd stared at so many times, where Nathan sat legs akimbo next to the manager, bulging manhood clear for all to see inside the royal blue club shorts, barely did him justice. Christ, it must have been at least eight inches. That wasn't a penis; it was a fucking truncheon. Life would never be the same again.

8

It was weird, thought Brooksy, flopping back on the sofa later that evening, how some days barely anything happened, then others were just rammed with news. He grabbed the TV remote and put his feet up on the coffee table.

News 24 was one rolling outdoors broadcast, flipping between reporters outside Marchmont, now cordoned off with police tape, the Prosperity Stadium and now - in the latest development - outside the house of Carey Hopkins' former PE teacher, Gregg Caine.

Brooksy focused on the Breaking News caption running across the bottom of the screen. *Greater Manchester Police have arrested the former PE teacher of Carey Hopkins, the 15 year old North West Rangers youth academy player who took his own life yesterday.*

He grabbed his phone and searched for further details on the BBC website. It was, unsurprisingly, the top story on both the News and Sports apps.

Gregg Caine, 32, was Hopkins' PE teacher at St Hubert's High School, Greater Manchester, where Carey was a pupil. Caine's contract was terminated by mutual consent by the oversubscribed Manchester high school last summer, for "personal reasons." However, a former school governor, who wishes to remain anonymous, has told the BBC that child pornography had been found on the popular PE teacher's laptop and allegations of male grooming made against him by several parents. It is thought that one of the images on Caine's computer featured

There did not appear to be any suggestion that Caine had any links with either Peter Byfield or Dennis Atkins, though. A surge of anger coloured Brooksy's cheeks. How the hell did sickos like that get to work with kids? Still, at least it took the heat off Rangers for now. He bet the club management were relieved. It didn't, of course, exonerate either Byfield or Atkins, but it at least diverted attention away from those two old dinosaurs in the every-shifting focus of 24/7 media.

St Hubert's High School, the article continued, had - in the words of its headteacher, Robert Wallasey-Price - contacted all pupils featured in the photographic images found on Caine's laptop. Forty-three boys were interviewed by specialist Child Liaison officers and Greater Manchester Police were satisfied that no improper behaviour had occurred between Mr Caine and underage boys, beyond storing images of them on his personal computer. It acknowledged that Mr Caine had not sought permission from parents before taking images of boys engaged in sporting pursuit for his own "teaching portfolio." However, another source informed the BBC that Caine was known to invite small groups of male pupils to stay behind for extra training sessions for football and athletics on a regular basis.

Bastard, Brooksy hissed. He'd read enough about the football abuse scandals in the press the last few years, to know that this was the paedos' standard method of enticing young lads into their sick lair - by playing on their desperation to succeed and capitalising on their naivety. Making them feel a cut above the rest for a fleeting moment in time, before cruelly destroying their lives forever with sexual violence against vulnerable young bodies and minds. Was this what had happened to Carey Hopkins? It seemed too much of a coincidence otherwise, Brooksy thought.

He felt sick, his recently digested ham and pasta salad threatening to make a reappearance. The TV screen flipped back from Caine's front door to the Prosperity Stadium, where it appeared Owen French had agreed to a brief interview.

Of course, whilst this does in no way excuse or exonerate any past employee of this club from unlawful and inappropriate behaviour, it does appear, if news reports are correct, that the club is not directly connected with whatever was troubling Carey. Nevertheless, this is a tragic event and our thoughts remain very much with the family and friends of Carey Hopkins, and the Club will continue to support our Academy trainees in this difficult time.

Smooth, if a little too quick to distance the club from Hopkins' suicide, Brooksy thought. The camera switched back to a staff photo of Caine, who looked like everyone's favourite PE teacher - young, good-looking and 'down with the kids,' complete with perfect teeth, lantern jaw, a quiffed forelock and New Armour trackies. Probably had the entire female staff and female pupils swooning after him - in vain.

Still, at least the attention - and with it, the whole media circus - would shift away from the club and onto Caine in his Oldham hideout. Hopefully things could return to some semblance of normality at the club and this sorry affair would all be forgotten. Brooksy checked himself. That was not a great attitude. Carey's death should not be in vain. Even if nobody at the club had been directly responsible for his suicide, they were still part of a wider culture that elevated the physically beautiful and athletically gifted, like Caine, and only asked character questions later, when it was often too late.

Brooksy turned the TV off. It was too easy to get sucked into the vortex of rolling news - especially when it was of a dark nature such as this - and find yourself dragged down with it.

♥♥♥♥♥

Nathan stretched out his toes and touched the end of the bathtub, enjoying the sensation of relaxing then tensing his muscles in the hot bubbly water. This king-size freestanding bath had been the investment of the century, as far as he was concerned. Alessandra was a fan, too, but tonight it was all his. He closed his eyes and sunk his tousled brown hair under the water. Aaah, that was good. It had been a horrible few days, but tonight he was determined to chill out.

His mind briefly switched to the embarrassing incident with Nick Brookes in physio that morning. Stop it! Nathan commanded himself out loud. It was nothing, no big deal, probably happened all the time. It was just a generic reaction to human touch, nothing to stress about. Brooksy hadn't even noticed, anyway, by the looks of it. He had already gone to fetch the heat spray.

Why did shameful or embarrassing incidents have a tendency to flash back across your mind at the most inopportune moments, Nathan wondered. If he told Alessandra, he knew she would hoot with laughter and tease him mercilessly. He was not prepared to revisit the incident on a daily basis, even if she would normalise it for him and put it in perspective.

Nathan lathered his muscular body with his favourite seaweed and elderflower bath gel and leaned back in the tub, staring at his patchwork reflection in the mirror tiles that scattered the wall and ceiling at random points, creating a shimmering effect in the expansive bathroom.

His phone bleeped with a text notification from the first team chat group. Europa League fixtures and travel dates. Nathan felt a frisson of excitement. Whilst it was a pain travelling to far off countries in the bowels of Europe, he could not deny there was something about playing elite European football that got his juices going. Nothing else came close, as far as Nathan was concerned - even going to fucking Bulgaria or Turkey, where half the team would get heckled on account of their skin colour, irrespective of their footballing talent. Perhaps he'd feel differently if he was black or Asian, Nathan pondered. It was not always easy to put yourselves in the shoes of other people, but we all had areas in which we felt judged or stigmatised in some context, and perhaps he needed to think how such instances made him feel. That would make a good team-talk exercise, Nathan thought.

He flickered through his social media quickly then put his phone back on the window ledge. He didn't want to read about Gregg Caine or St Hubert's High. The club would do something to respect Carey's memory - a charity game or some such. Then the club would move on. Byfield and Atkins would be consigned to the murky past and North West would retain its glossy modern image.

9

"Ok, a bit of silence, please!" Johnny Ziegler hollered in the players' restaurant at the now reopened Marchmont training complex. The first team and reserves gradually ceased their banter and sat to attention.

"Our next preseason friendly is, as you know, next Tuesday night in Sofia. The flight is only two hours, so no need to travel before Tuesday. We'll be leaving from Manchester on the 8.40 flight, please assemble at the Stadium for 6.00 am."

Groans arose from the teenage members of the squad. Nathan and Tango grinned at each other, used to such reactions as the elder statesmen of a team with an average age of 24, the youngest of the top six in the British Premier League.

"There will be a light lunch and training session at the actual stadium, followed by a period of rest at our hotel, which is just a short ride away."

"Johnny, isn't Bulgaria where they abused the England lads a few years back?" Dazzer queried.

Ziegler nodded. "Yes, Daz. So, management have already formulated a media statement that will be issued at our press conference. It says that the club will not tolerate racism of any kind and will be liaising with the UEFA officials to employ all appropriate measures if required - even in a friendly."

"Including leaving the pitch?" Tango asked.

"Of course," Ziegler nodded in confirmation. He looked around him. Some of the black lads clearly looked anxious, while others rolled their eyes at one another in tired frustration at the sheer ridiculousness that such an issue should still exist in the 21st century. He made a note to have a 121 with Chas, Jordan and Sav at some point, without embarrassing the lads. It was a sensitive subject. Some liked to own their ethnicity very publicly, for others it was not something they wanted to draw particular attention to, as some kind of master status.

"Oi, Panko!" Tango called down the table to his teammate. "You knocked your snoring on the head yet, mate?"

Pankhurst's wife's various attempts to curb her husband's snoring was the subject of much mirth among the first team. Panko responded with a middle finger salute.

"It's alright for you, Tang, you don't have to share a bleedin' room with him," Jordan Morrison groaned.

"No, I'm only stuck with young Tom Jones here this this season, aren't I?" Tango grinned, slapping Huw Simons on the back. "Probably keep me awake singing all night!"

"It's called mentoring the kids, Tango, so make sure you set a good example," Nathan grinned.

"That's right, make me sound like a bloody paedo!"

There was nervous laughter around the room.

"Nah, you've got no chance there, mate," Dazzer cackled. "One cop of your ginger pubes and the kid would run a fuckin' mile!" The gallows humour relieved the tension. Nathan guffawed.

"It's aw'right for you, pal," Tango grumbled, "you get a swanky big room all to yourself, you fucker!"

"Captain's prerogative, mate," Nathan laughed,

getting up with his tray. It was too glorious a day to sit indoors a moment longer. He was glad he'd had the foresight to sling his mountain bike in the back of the jeep earlier than morning. Time to hit the trail.

♥♥♥♥♥

The woodland felt gloriously cool after Nathan's physical exertions on the training ground that morning.He stood up in the saddle to begin the slow ascent uphill on his favoured black mountain bike, his tall, muscular frame now encased in a navy-blue Lycra one piece, with yellow cycling shoes to match his cycle helmet. He stopped at the top of the clearing, breathing in the refreshing piney air and listening to the birds in the treesand the distant sound of a cricket. The trials and tribulations of North West Rangers felt a million miles away as he decided which path to take from his vantage point. It was not too hot, and he had plenty fluids with him. He could afford to take the longer of the three available routes.

The path was mazy and narrow and followed an undulating course. A gentle breeze tickled his face as Nathan weaved and sped in and out of the greenery. It was good to be away from it all.

One of the perks of being an elite footballer was having most afternoons free. For all the stresses and media nonsense that went with the job, Nathan could not deny the hours were good. Not for him loafing around at home watching Netflix or playing Fifa, though. When this gig was over, he planned on devoting his time to something outdoorsy. Cycling or kayaking or another of

61

his favourite hobbies that currently played second fiddle to football. In the winter, he'd take to the ski slopes, an activity strictly forbidden for a top professional footballer on account of the potential danger to the knees and ankles.

Nathan had no desire to take his coaching badges at this moment in time. Whilst he was an intelligent footballer, he disliked the limelight and hoped to slip into some semblance of normal life once his legs went. Hopefully the end of his playing career was still a decade or so away, though. Maybe he'd trot off to the States in his mid-thirties and get a gig with some fancy pants American franchise. Not for him slumming it in the lower leagues of British football, getting his head kicked in by some overambitious journeyman on a semi-frozen pitch in Accrington.

Just under two hours later, Nathan pushed his bike down the final prohibitively steep incline toward the carpark. A dark blue Golf was pulling into the otherwise deserted carpark. Nathan kept his bike helmet on for an instant and turned his back on the new arrival. He was easily recognisable and the helmet at least afforded some disguise. However, his NH6 number plate was an immediate giveaway, at least to someone who parked in its vicinity on a daily basis.

"You again!" Brooksy laughed, stuffing his car keys and phone into a hydration pack and tightening the backpack around his body.

Nathan turned around, slightly sheepishly. It was physio guy again, in tiny little blue running shorts and a white vest top, showing off his compactly muscled legs and torso.

"Hi Brooksy. I see we had the same idea - well, get away from it all, that is. I brought my bike." Well that was kinda obvious, Nathan chastised himself inwardly. What a berk.

"So I see," Brooksy smiled. He whistled. "Nice bike."

"Yeah, it's my favourite mountain bike," Nathan replied.

"You have a collection then?"

Nathan indicated his head affirmatively. "Just a couple of mountains. Got a road bike, too, and a Fat Tyres."

"Oh yeah, they're great fun!" Brooksy laughed convivially.

"Bloody expensive though!" Nathan nodded again, unsure of how to respond.

"Well, not for you, obviously," Brooksy grinned, echoing Nathan's thoughts.

"Do you ride?" Nathan asked, steering the conversation away from his obvious wealth.

"Yeah, I bring the bike up here," Brooksy replied. "If you meant bikes?"

Nathan laughed. "Think you might struggle to get a horse in a Golf, mate."

Brooksy chuckled. "You'd be surprised what I can get in Tiger with the back seats down."

"Tiger?"

"Yano, Woods. Golf."

Nathan shook his head in mock despair.

"We should take the bikes out one day together," Brooksy commented, tightening the straps of his hydration pack and trying to look nonchalant.

"Could do," Nathan replied slowly. "Gets kinda boring sometimes doing stuff on my tod. Rest of the guys have either got kids or act like big kids, sitting on their sodding Playstations all afternoon and evening."

"Yeah, know what you mean," Brooksy nodded. "Not my idea of fun, either."

"We should do it then," Nathan smiled. "Any afternoon after training works for me - unless we have a game the next day. Gotta conserve my energy in my old age and all that!"

"Yeah, most afternoons are fine for me too," Brooksy concurred. "I have some induction stuff at the moment - had to stay behind today - but should be done with that soon."

"It's a plan, then," Nathan said and high-fived the smaller man with a cycling gloved right hand.

10

Did that really just happen? Brooksy grinned to himself, setting off on a gentle jog through the woodland. Like Nathan before him, the cool forest air was a welcome tonic from the baking sun that had beat down on them during training at the Prosperity that morning.

He'd slipped that in quite naturally, Brooksy thought, the invite to join him for bike ride. Not too pushy, not too obvious, even if it had taken every ounce of his concentration not to stare at the very obvious bulge in Nathan's Lycra one piece.

As with a run through the forest in the late summer heat, Brooksy knew he would need to pace himself in his exchanges with Nathan Hunt. One betrayal of his attraction to the Rangers skipper and Hunt would scarper. Nathan was not the type to talk shit about anyone, Brooksy knew that. But he was cool and reserved and unlikely to associate with anyone who would embarrass him in any way, of that Brooksy was certain. He'd done his homework on Hunt, on being given the vacant physio post at North West with the acrimonious departure of Dennis Atkins. Brooksy's self-tuition had included an old YouTube clip of an interview on Football Focus with Hunt. The guy had made Shearer look like the village gossip in comparison, so short, measured and neutral had he been in his responses to the female interviewer's probing questions. She had clearly had a big fat crush on Hunt, too, Brooksy had noted. But then you could hardly blame her, could you, sat opposite this well-built, well-endowed man, so quietly controlled and self-confident.

Brooksy admired that in Nathan, even if it would probably drive you made in real life. Especially if you were in a relationship with…. Stop it! Brooksy shook his head as he sped up to a brisker jog, the dry twigs cracking under the steady thwack of his trainers as he pounded a path through the mazy woodland, his white shirted torso appearing and disappearing in the intermittent sunlight.

♥♥♥♥♥

The period of respite for North West Rangers was soon over. Gregg Caine had links to Peter Byfield through the local schools' football scouting programme. Texts from Caine had been found on Byfield's iPhone, containing photos of 'promising lads' from St Hubert's and its primary feeder schools, some of the kids as young as 9 and 10. Byfield might like to take an interest in these kids, was the not so innocent suggestion implied in the messages.

All these texts had been sent in the past two years, while Caine was employed at St Hubert's, and Byfield still employed by Rangers. There was no shirking the club's link with a potential child sex abuse ring now.

Nathan threw his shoes at the TV in physical revulsion as the SkyNews reporter appeared suitably sombre outside the iron gates of the Prosperity Stadium. He genuinely cared about the club and desperately did not want its growing reputation sullied by this whole revolting business.

"Penny for them?" Alessandra commented, folding

her long legs under her as she resumed her usual spot on the armchair opposite Nathan.

"That PE teacher is connected to Byfield through some fuckin' paedo ring," Nathan grunted.

"And?" Alessandra frowned.

"And that means it's not historical, because he was sending Byfield pictures of schoolkids recently."

"So, it is linked to the club?"

Nathan nodded grimly. Alessandra let out a long, low whistle. "That's not good."

"It's a fucking nightmare," Nathan growled and consulted his phone. He was needed for a Facetime with management in twenty minutes. Sometimes being club captain was more hassle than it was worth. At many clubs, the first team lived in a bubble, protected from the outside world as far as possible. Not at Rangers, where players, particularly the senior pros, were encouraged to hobnob with the management and youth team alike, to create the family atmosphere the club's Spanish manager so highly rated. For the most part, it was a profitable strategy, in Nathan's view. Whilst it was way too early in the fledgling club's history to speak of individual team loyalty, the players certainly felt their views counted. The manager and first team coach team, Jantzen and Ziegler, commanded enormous respect among the first team squad, precisely because they did listen to the players. They hadn't just rocked up and imposed a strategical straitjacket on the team, as many overseas management combos seemed to do these days, in Nathan's view, killing the spirit of a club.

The downside of being viewed as such an integral part of Rangers, though, was being dragged into some of the seamier aspects of club life. However, this affair had to be the worst he'd experienced in nearly three years at North West. Spats between players and missed drug tests paled into comparison with this tragic - and now vile - business.

Nathan scrolled down on his screen, reading a long email from Owen French, director of the club. It looked like the training ground would be closed again the next day while specially trained police officers interviewed the whole youth academy about any contact young players might have had with either Peter Byfield or Gregg Caine. Despite the usual claims that the police were keeping an open mind, it seemed the assumption was that Carey Hopkins had taken his own life in relation to abuse at the hands of these men, given his links to St Hubert's High and local ties. Hopefully, they would get the information they required to lock the monsters up, and everyone could just move on and focus on football again. He walked across to Alessandra and held his arms out for a hug. She obliged. He stroked her hair, holding her close, suddenly feeling the need for some human consolation.

11

"Bad day?" Alessandra asked, opening the front door into the capacious hallway just after 5pm the following afternoon. Nathan grunted, throwing his holdall across the marble floor.

She followed him into the kitchen. "I prepared dinner for you. I have a network meeting, but I thought you wouldn't be in the mood for cooking."

"Thanks," Nathan nodded, kissing the top of her dark head. "Sorry to be mardy. It's all a bit grim."

"With the police?"

"Yep. They headed our way in the afternoon, in case any of the younger guys in the first team knew anything."

Alessandra frowned. "That suggests they didn't find what they were looking for with the kids."

Nathan shrugged. "Who knows?" He wandered into the downstairs closet to take a pee. "I just wanna get back playing, you know?"

"Aren't you away soon for the Champions Cup?"

"Europa League," Nathan corrected her, washing his hands as Alessandra was there. "Not for a while yet. But we have a friendly in Bulgaria the week after next."

"Nice!" she snorted in a derisory way.

"It's a distraction from this shit," Nathan shrugged, wandering back into the kitchen.

"'Spose," Alessandra replied, clearly not convinced. Whilst she appreciated the lifestyle of the elite footballer, she couldn't pretend to find the game itself enthralling, with its insane media exposure and its preening self-obsessed players. At least Nathan wasn't like that. He was mature, measured, cool as a cucumber and down to earth - though not in that crass, crude way that was so typical of the archetypal British male. And great eye candy for the discerning woman, as well, Alessandra thought to herself. She felt proud to wear Nathan Hunt on her arm at top gala events. He had a continental air that was missing in so many British men, with his well-trimmed dark beard and penchant for expensive designer suits.

"Perhaps you should go out later," Alessandra shrugged. "Hanging round here all evening on your own is maybe not a good idea. And for fuck sake, don't put the TV on. It's full of it."

"Mm, that sounds like a plan," Nathan mused, grabbing an iced water from the dispenser on the fridge door. He took out his phone and went to the first team chat. Were the physios on there?

♥♥♥♥♥

"Lovely evening for it," Brooksy smiled, slapping the top of his saddle as he welcomed Nathan in the carpark.

Nathan smiled, extricating his bike from the back of the Jeep.

"Looks like we're gonna have a beautiful sunset tonight," Brooksy continued, nodding towards the sky, already showing streaks of orange in the mixed blue hues that September evening.

"It's just good to get away from it all," Nathan remarked, putting his feet on the lip of the boot to change out of his trainers into his fluorescent yellow mountain bike shoes.

"Fucking awful day."

"Yeah, the police talked to me too. I guess I worked with the kids for a few weeks."

"They weren't interested in me, but the younger kids got pulled in - well not Bolz or Huwsy, obviously, but all the local guys."

"So, how'd you get my number?" Brooksy enquired, wisely changing the subject, to avoid spoiling the serenity of the late summer woodland setting.

"You've been added to the Whatsapp group - for the travel plans to Bulgaria, I guess."

"Have I?" Brooksy asked, barely able to contain his pleasure. Unbelievable though it was, he, Nick Brookes, was part of the first team set-up at footballing giants, North West Rangers.

Nathan declined to mention that he had personally asked Johnny to do so, purely for physio related communications, of course.

Nathan shrugged with fake nonchalance. "You're part of the crew now, aren't you? Luisa's on there - poor girl. Fuck knows what she thinks of half the shit posted on there."

"I think she would cope just fine, from what I've seen of her," Brooksy laughed as they pushed their bikes towards the opening to the bridle path, that would take them around the far perimeter of the country park, away from members of the public taking a gentle evening stroll.

"I didn't think we'd meet up so soon," Brooksy continued. Nathan didn't say much. He wasn't one to initiate conversations, Brooksy had noticed that from the few dealings he'd had with him thus far. Still, it had been Nathan who had proposed the bike ride tonight, to switch off from a dark day. It seemed he was a man of action, not of words. And there was no problem with that, Brooksy thought to himself. Just so long as he, Brooksy, was prepared to do the talking. But not too much of it -Nathan struck Brooksy as someone who would quickly become irritated with pointless small talk.

"Ali suggested it," Nathan replied a few moments later. "Thought it wasn't a good idea to hang around by myself all evening. She's got one of her network things. Fuck knows what she does there. Sounds boring as hell."

"I wouldn't knock it, mate," Brooksy laughed. "Your girlfriend's doing pretty well for herself. Least you know she's not after you for your money."

Nathan didn't correct him. Alessandra wasn't his girlfriend, she was…. how to categorise their relationship? It was a complicated thing, but it worked at this point in time. Neither of them wanted to live in each other's pockets but appreciated the company on a regular basis. Nathan couldn't be bothered to explain it and he barely knew Brooksy, in any case.

"Do you want to take the lead?" Nathan suggested. "You're more familiar with this route than I am, I think."

"Sure," Brooksy replied. "You might wanna keep a few feet back. There's a few points where I know it gets kind of hairy and I might slow down suddenly."

Shame, Brooksy thought to himself. I don't get to look at his arse. He took a sneaky sidelong appraising glance at Nathan, dressed this time in separates and not the skin-tight all in one piece from the other day. His firm muscles and sizeable assets were still clearly visible below the black Lycra, however. Brooksy wanted to pinch himself. Was this real? Here he was, recently qualified physio, hanging out with the great Nathan Hunt, of North West Rangers and the GB national squad, Captain Marvel and defensive man mountain, plus every footballing cliché in between.

But he had to be careful not to show either deferential or lustful feelings towards Hunt. Brooksy knew neither would hold much truck with the older man, who was ostensibly as straight as a die, in every sense of the word. It was ok. He could play it cool. Brooksy had long since learned that communicating a measured and mature air got you places, even if his heart was beating furiously below the confident exterior.

After some forty minutes in the saddle, Brooksy suddenly became aware that Nathan was not behind him. He stopped and turned his blonde head, sweaty tendrils of his forelock peeping out below his navy-blue helmet. He could see the yellow of Nathan's headwear about twenty yards back through the trees. He cycled slowly back to him.

"What's up?"

"Got something going on with my gears," Nathan replied, bent over his bike.

Brooksy dismounted. "Let's have a look." He squatted down and fiddled with the gear mechanism on Nathan's bike. "You've got a tiny stone wedged in the sprockets by the looks of it."

"Yeah, that's what I thought was causing it, but my car keys are too blunt to get it out. I have plenty gear in the car, of course."

"But we're miles away, yeah," Brooksy agreed. He stood up and unzipped his bumbag. "Good job I've always got this with me, then." He pulled out a micro screwdriver.

"For fuck sake, you're serious about this, aren't you mate?" Nathan grinned.

Brooksy shrugged. "It's not like it takes up any room, you wouldn't believe how many times lil' screwy has come in handy!"

"Don't go fucking saying that on the Whatsapp group," Nathan laughed. "You'll never live it down."

He looks gorgeous when he laughs, Brooksy thought. Nathan's normally sullen face lit up totally, taking years off him. He tried to keep his eyes off the sizeable bulge in Nathan's cycling shorts, just a foot or so away from him the other side of the bike, as he prized the tiny stone out of the gear shaft. The guy clearly dressed to the right... stop it! Nathan felt himself hardening. Fortunately, as with carrying a mini screwdriver in his bumbag, Brooksy had come prepared, making sure he wore a loose-fitting t-shirt over his navy-blue cycle shorts.

"Gotcha!" Brooksy exclaimed, easing the stone out finally. He held it up in the palm of his hand for Nathan to see. "Amazing that something that small can stop you in your tracks - literally."

"They're delicate machines, these top-notch bikes," Nathan commented. "Thanks, mate."

He smiled at Brooksy, who smiled back. It was what you called a moment of male bonding, Brooksy supposed. In hetero world, anyway. Was this going to develop into a bromance of sorts?

"So," Nathan began, getting back on the saddle right at Brooksy's eye level, who was bent down, adjusting the straps on his shoes. Brooksy caught his breath and turned his back hastily on Nathan, less he gave himself away. "Onwards and upwards!"

"Quite literally," Brooksy replied. "The next bit's a bugger, but then we get an amazing view at the top over the valley. Especially with these skies tonight. Then it's pretty much downhill all the way."

"Lead on, then," Nathan smiled, relieved that he didn't have to push his bike back some two miles or so back to the carpark.

♥♥♥♥♥

Brooksy lay back naked under the single white sheet that night, a broad smile across his face. Who would have thought that such an unpleasant day could have ended so … beautifully. Because there was no other word for it - it had truly been a beautiful experience, spending an evening in the forest with Nathan Hunt on a warm summer evening under that sky. They had stood together at the top, surveying the valley below, pointing out the Stadium and the city limits. Perspective had been regained after the trials of a day held hostage to Greater Manchester Police.

His hand strayed under the duvet and he took his penis in his hand. Though his body ached from the physical exertion of a five-mile bike ride in hilly terrain, his brain was wired and sexual feelings raced through his bloodstream like some kind of internal car chase. He knew he wouldn't sleep without some holistic activity

75

that engaged all of his senses. Nathan Hunt in Lycra adjusting his saddle position consumed Brooksy's thoughts as he pleasured himself to sleep.

12

That felt better, Nathan thought inwardly, jogging backwards to the six yard box, having diagonally crossed a ball inch-perfect to the feet of Timo Bolz, who was at this very second bombing down the left-wing to the by-line, where he would undoubtedly whip one of his beauties towards the incoming head of Jordan Morrison.

He clenched a fist as Morrison's thumping header escaped the clutches of reserve keeper, Luke Shilling, into the roof of the net. It was only a training game, but a pretty meaty one at that. It seemed the whole squad was only too eager to put a horrible week behind them and focus on what they did best - chasing a small spherical leather item around a grassy rectangle. It was crazy, really, when you took a step back and thought about it, Nathan often pondered in one of his many reflective moments - though not quite as daft as launching an aerodynamic spear heavenwards, or four grown men running round in Lycra hot suits passing a metal tube to one another in track and field!

He squinted his eyes as the sun beat down relentlessly on the now re-opened Marchmont training pitch. He was looking forward to their first Champions League adventure of the season. The plans had been changed, so that they were now travelling to Sofia the day before. Nathan was pleased about that. It was always better to have a relaxed morning prior to a match, rather than charging around on the actual day. He found he rarely slept well when he knew he had to be up early, and consequently felt shattered by the time the match started. He could think of at least one far off foray to Eastern or

Southern Europe where he'd had a shocker by his high standards owing to fatigue.

The two teams in the 'friendly' training game were more than a little mismatched, Nathan thought, as Dazzer this time sent a cross flying from the right wing towards Morrison in the far goalmouth. It was already three nil to the green bibs. It wasn't the most taxing match ever, for himself and the green bib defence. Hence he had plenty time to consider the scratches down his calves from the bike ride with Brooksy the other night. It had been fun, even if Alessandra had commented that he looked like he'd had a fight with a herd of cats rather than taken a bike ride with a friend. Friend… was Brooksy a friend?

He shielded his dark brown eyes with his right hand as he looked up the pitch to where Brooksy was dealing with a cramp stricken Sav Johal. That didn't bode well, so early in the season. Looked like the kid had got a bit out of shape over the summer break. It was a hot day, but hardly baking.

Nathan didn't have many friends besides Alessandra. In truth, he didn't really feel the need for them. Club duties and fitness training took up the vast majority of his time, and when he did have down time, kayaking and road cycling were his big hobbies. Nathan had never been one for hanging out in bars or clubs. He hated feeling out of control in any way and he had too much self-respect for himself, or women, to engage in one-night stands.

But he couldn't deny, it had felt nice having company on the bike ride. Brooksy was easy to be around and didn't force conversation on Nathan. He was way more grown up than most of the guys his age on the playing staff. Maybe it was because Brooksy wasn't earning stupid money, had to take care of himself, rather than being the mollycoddled babies most of the guys were. Was he any different, Nathan wondered. He pretty much took care of his own shit. Ali helped out a bit and a cleaner and gardener came in. And he had his PA. But other than that, Nathan reckoned he was pretty self-contained.

Maybe he'd arrange another bike ride or a run with Brooksy soon. The guy seemed pretty discreet, not the type to post shit all over social media about them hanging out together.

Flurgghh… Nathan felt his forehead hit the deck as he was uprooted by a clumsy challenge from red-bibbed squad player, Petter Lindstrom.

"Sorry, mate," Lindstrom apologised, holding his hand out to help his club captain up.

Cocky little fucker, Nathan growled inwardly, declining the young Swede's hand and getting up by himself. He'd lost concentration there for a second. Not good.

♥♥♥♥♥

Despite drubbing the Red Bibs 6-2, Nathan's mood had darkened by the time he entered the changing room. He was cross he'd let two goals in, which while technically not his fault, Nathan still took as a personal affront. Ultra competitive and even more self-critical, Nathan prided himself on marshalling a fortress style defence, whatever the occasion, whatever the human makeup of this defensive line. Clean sheets were his specialty.

"He's pretty sharp, that Linda," Tango commented, sensing the cause of Nathan's dark mood.

"Needs to improve his touch, though," Nathan replied rather uncharitably with regard to Petter Lindstrom.

Tango laughed. "That wouldn't have anything to do with him leaving you flat on your arse, would it?"

Nathan just grunted and pulled his sweaty training top off.

"Dirk whatshisname did well, looks useful in the holding role," Tango continued.

"Van Huizen," Nathan corrected him. He was good with names - always a useful trait in a club captain.

"Aaah, gerroff me, you fuckin' paedo!" Dazzer yelled suddenly above the ubiquitous drum and bass music that pumped out in the changing room.

Nathan turned round sharply to see Darren Petrie holding Timo Bolz in an arm lock.

"I'll mess yer hair up, you woofter," Dazzer mock-threatened his German team-mate, a big grin across his acne-ridden face.

"I'll pop your zits, Pizza boy," Timo retorted unwisely. He had picked up the vernacular quickly.

"Touché!" Tango hooted as Dazzer released Timo and gave him an almighty shove across the training room.

"Just get in the shower," Nathan growled, as Bolz crashed into his legs.

"What's your problem?" Tango enquired of Nathan. Nathan ignored him and headed for the showers. Tango shrugged and followed suit.

♥♥♥♥♥

"What's up with you?" Alessandra queried, as she pulled up in the expansive gravel pathway of Nathan's glass-fronted property. She could tell by his furrowed brow that he was in pissed-off mode.

She smacked his butt playfully as she stood beside him.

"Don't we have a sprinkler to do that?" she asked, watching him hose down a bed of colourful flowers.

"They need drowning in this heat," Nathan grunted.

"Want to talk about it?" she enquired.

"Not really," Nathan replied, looking straight ahead. Alessandra shrugged. She wasn't going to push it. It could be anything with Nathan. He wasn't exactly an open book and she didn't have the energy to prize it out of him that evening. This heat was exhausting, even for an Italian.

Nathan turned the hose off and left it in place for the next morning. He went indoors.

"You're not joining me for dinner?" Alessandra wondered, as Nathan reappeared a few minutes later in running shorts and a vest. He shook his head.

"Leave some for me, I'm off for a run."

"Clearly," Alessandra replied dryly and watched him tie the laces of his running shoes. The sparsely dotted residents of the exclusive suburb were used to seeing Rangers' captain pounding the tarmac and blessedly left him in peace.

That's better, Nathan thought, setting off at a rather ambitious pace, given the humidity. But he just needed to let out the frustrations of the day; his body had felt propelled towards taking physical action to crush the rising demons inside.

13

"So where are we staying tonight, boss?" Tango asked Nathan, as he stretched the seatbelt fabric to fit around his considerable frame on the Sofia bound chartered airplane that following Monday evening.

"Don't you ever read Johnny's texts?" Nathan grumbled.

"Not if I can just ask you instead," Tango grinned, fiddling with the TV console.

"It's called the Sense Hotel, based on Sofia's most exclusive boulevard," Nathan read from his phone.

"Well that's no use for Tango, on both counts!" Dazzer chortled from the seat behind.

"Shut up, Marge," Tango retorted, who had taken to called Darren Petrie 'Marge' - short for Margherita, not Margarita - on account of his unfortunate complexion. "Is it really called the Sense Hotel?"

Nathan showed him his phone. "Look!"

Several rows back, Brooksy smiled at the exchange. Though he'd never admit it to anyone, except perhaps his ma and pa, this had to be one of the most exciting experiences of his 22 year old life so far. It was hard to fathom that he, Nick Brookes, was sat aboard a flight abroad with the first team of North West Rangers, just a few rows back from German hotshot and teen magazine icon, Timo Bolz, and defensive stalwarts of the British game, Nathan Hunt and James 'Tango' Mackay.

He tried to concentrate as Luisa ran through their schedule for the next day in Sofia, but his head remained staunchly above the clouds.

♥♥♥♥♥

Tango whistled as they milled in the foyer of the five star Sense Hotel in the heart of Sofia. It wasn't bad, to be fair, and the pool looked promising. Shame they were only here for one night, but it was one night more than was originally planned.

"What's the hold-up?" Jordan asked Tango, whom he knew had the ear of the captain, who was currently engaged in a rather heated conversation with Johnny Ziegler and a young female concierge and an older man in a suit, who was presumably the manager.

"They've cocked the rooms up, apparently, put Luisa and Brooksy in together, either didn't realise Luisa wasn't Luis or Nick wasn't Nicola," Tango laughed.

"Ha, the problems of foreign travel!" Dazzer giggled. "Lucky Brooksy!"

Tango made a face. "I'd say lucky Luisa. She's no looker."

"That's a bit Inverdale, Tango my lad," Aston Rideout, the keeper, chastised him.

"But true!" Dazzer laughed.

"She gives you a run for the money with the old Zit Stick, doesn't she, Daz?" Jordan Morrison cawed, slapping Petrie's skinny back.

"Fuck off, Mozza," Dazzer retorted.

"So what's occurrin', boss man?" Tango enquired, as Nathan walked towards them.

"Luisa's got the room to herself, they're putting Brooksy in with me," Nathan replied. "They're full, some big trade event."

"So, you don't get your bed all to yourself for once?"

84

Tango grinned.

"It's a twin double, isn't it, arsehole," Nathan replied. "Anyone know where the physios are? Need to break the sad news they're not shacking up tonight."

"Don't think Brooksy will be too bothered, mate," Jordan commented. Nathan shot him a sidelong glance. What was he insinuating? Nathan had not been party to the disparaging comments on Luisa's facial acne a few moments ago.

"Better hope he doesn't snore, wouldn't want anyone to destroy your beauty sleep before the big name against Sporting Whatever!" Tango laughed.

"Yeah, well, it's only one night," Nathan replied testily.

Fuckin' hell, he's irritable, Tango thought to himself. He'd have to keep an eye on his defensive partner in the game. Nathan had a habit of sliding in on opponents and giving away cheap yellow cards when he was in one of his dark moods. It was only a preseason friendly, but Tango wouldn't want Nathan picking up some stupid self-inflicted injury right before the Community Shield final at Wembley the following Sunday. It might only be for charity, but there wasn't a single player at North West who didn't want to put one over rivals City.

"So, guys," Johnny Ziegler chipped in, breaking into the huddle of players in the hotel foyer. "Downtime for two hours. Take a nap, or a splash in the pool, whatever takes your fancy and is relaxing for you, but please stay in the hotel. Supper is at 7pm, then the gaffer wants a word at about half eight. We head straight to the stadium for training after breakfast tomorrow."

There were grunts of approval as Johnny handed out

their room passes.

As was his custom, as much for the brief respite it offered him, as the fitness benefits, Nathan took the stairs to his fourth-floor room. As things went, it could have been a whole lot worse than sharing with Brooksy. Whilst he didn't know him so well as his teammates, at least he wasn't annoying like most of them. Hopefully he didn't grind his teeth or snore, or perform any of the other nocturnal physical ticks that might put Nathan off his A-game.

♥♥♥♥♥

"Ah, there you are," Nathan commented, lowering himself into the shallow end of the large pool, where Brooksy was leaning back on the tiled surround, eyes shut. "Been looking for you."

Brooksy opened his eyes and turned his head, to be greeted with the sight of Nathan Hunt naked but for a pair of black drawstring swim shorts. This day just gets better, Brooksy thought to himself, unaware of what was just about to come.

Brooksy began to regret wearing a pair of figure-hugging blue boardies, as he felt his blood pressure rise. Best keep his lower half below sea level. Even with baggy swim shorts on, Nathan's manhood was clear to see. Nathan had clearly not adopted the angst-ridden teenage boy habit of wearing restrictive boxers below the swim shorts to keep the tackle under control. Or maybe the netting just didn't chafe.

"Where's Luisa?" Nathan enquired, flipping over onto his back and taking in the ceiling of the swimming pool. Brooksy tried to avert his gaze from the bulge in the older man's shorts, now more obvious below the wet fabric.

"Gone to inspect the gym," Brooksy replied. "You were looking for me?"

Nathan stood up and swept the moisture back from his face. Fuck, you are beautiful, Brooksy thought inwardly, taking in Nathan's broad shoulders, observing how the dark hair at the base of his neck spread across his pecs then narrowly down his stomach, stopping tantalisingly short at the top of his swim shorts.

"They cocked up the rooms," Nathan replied, squinting. "Ouch, bit too much chlorine in this pool."

"I don't think so," Brooksy replied coolly. "Maybe you're just sensitive to it?"

I like that, Nathan thought. He has the guts to disagree with me, instead of agreeing and fawning all over me like most of the players - well except for Tango, of course, who had no qualms about putting Nathan in his place.

"So, what's with the rooms?" Brooksy enquired, returning to the subject in hand.

"Yeah. Basically - this is kinda funny, I guess - they booked Luisa in as Luis. Assumed she was a man, being a physio for us, so they put you in one room, which is obviously not on."

Brooksy decided it was probably not in his interests to mention his sexuality and that, actually, it wasn't such a big deal!

"So, in a nutshell, the hotel is fully booked for some European trade thing and the only spare bed is in my room, cos I normally get a twin room to myself -

captain's privilege."

Brooksy felt his heartrate triple instantly. "Sure, no prob," he shrugged nonchalantly. "Unless you snore, that is?"

Fucking cheek! Nathan thought to himself. The lad ought to be bowing and scraping in gratitude that he was sacrificing his much sought-after solitude to give him a bed for the night. Not that all clubs offered their captains this perk - but it was one that Nathan had gratefully accepted. He needed his personal space.

"Great, that's sorted then," Nathan replied and watched as Brooksy pushed himself off the tiled wall and launched himself into a powerful front crawl. He's one fit guy, Nathan thought to himself.

<h1 style="text-align:center">14</h1>

"Hey," Brooksy murmured sleepily as Nathan considerately let himself quietly into their room at a quarter past eleven that evening. Brooksy had long since gone to bed, being quarter past midnight in reality for them. It had been a long day and he was by habit, early to bed, early to rise.

"I was trying not to wake you, mate," Nathan said, taking his watch off and placing on the beside cabinet.

"Don't worry, I wasn't really asleep," Brooksy lied. "Did you have a meeting or something?"

"Not really," Nathan replied, stripping down to a pair of white trunks that stood out in the inky darkness. Brooksy would have loved to have turned the light on for a better view of Nathan in the nearly-buff. "I was just chatting to the new boys, the Dutch lad, Linda and Huwsy. Captain's duties and all that."

"You can turn the light on, if you want," Brooksy offered, feigning casualness.

"Sure? Thanks. Didn't have time to unpack earlier, I'll be furtling around in the dark for my toothbrush forever at this rate."

Nathan turned the light on next to his double bed, and Brooksy took the opportunity, while Nathan had his back to him, to take in the older man's suntanned, well-muscled and not overly hirsute 6ft 3' body. He didn't have a single tattoo, Brooksy noted. That was unusual in most guys these days, and especially for a footballer. He didn't have any kids, true. Maybe Alessandra didn't mean that much. It certainly didn't seem to be a particularly committed relationship. Nathan didn't seem   the marrying type to Brooksy. Far too fond of his own company. He was probably the most self-contained guy Brooksy had ever come across. He was pretty independent himself, but Nathan took it to a whole new level.

Still, most lads still had a tattoo of something, even if it was just a favourite team or close family member. Brooksy himself had his late grandad's initials on his wrist.

He looked the other way quickly as Nathan turned round to walk over to the bathroom. The skin-tight white trunks certainly showed off Nathan's manhood to its full advantage. What Brooksy would do to slide his hand inside the open fly and cop a feel of that dick. It was probably the most famous bulge in the whole football league, and he, Nick Brookes, was lying just metres away from it!

Forgetting that he was sharing a room, Nathan did not bother shutting the bathroom door, allowing Brooksy a full view of him taking a pee. It was fucking massive, Brooksy thought, not for the first time.

He watched Nathan's right scapula move as he brushed his teeth. His back was hairless, Brooksy observed. Hairy backs grossed him out. Perhaps it was something to do with the added pubes in the shower? Brooksy was fastidious about cleanliness. A hairy bathroom - or physio room, for that matter - was probably top of his list of bugbears, alongside egomaniacs and drunken women. Unfortunately, the latter two were very much in evidence in the world of elite footballers.

"Mind if I turn the aircon off and open the windows?"

Nathan asked, turning the bathroom light off and returning to the bedroom. "The aircon kills my throat."

"Sure," Brooksy replied, not feeling he could really object in the circumstances. The whirring on and off annoyed him anyway.

"Breakfast is at 8, I'll set my alarm for 7.30," Nathan commented, kicking out at the hospital corners on his bedding so that he could stretch his feet out in bed.

"I've already set mine for 6.30," Brooksy replied, yawning. "Wanna go out for a run or something first. I'm going to be sat around much more than you guys tomorrow."

"Yeah," Nathan replied and turned the beside lamp off. Brooksy could see the white light of his phone in the darkness. The voile curtain over the open windows blew gently in the tiny breeze in the late July air.

Brooksy closed his eyes and tried to focus himself to sleep, but this was not going to be easy. He'd shared a room plenty of times, obviously, his bed on a frequent basis, but not with this degree of unresolved sexual tension in the air - on his part, of course.

Finally, the exertions of the day and the lethargizing effects of travel caught up with, and nullified, the tension in his body and Brooksy drifted off into sleep.

Finished with his usual bedtime telephonic ablutions, Nathan doublechecked his alarm was set, and put his phone down on the bedside table to charge overnight. He looked across the room to where the younger man was obviously now asleep on his back, his steady breathing gently audible alongside the gentle tickling of the curtains in the wind.

Nathan's gaze lingered a moment on the blonde

physio. He was a good-looking bloke. Slightly shorter than average height, maybe, but toned and fit-looking - as you would expect for a physio, of course. He hadn't mentioned a girlfriend, but Nathan was sure he couldn't be short of offers. Brooksy kept his cards close to his chest, though; Nathan had noted that in the brief period of their acquaintance. Maybe that's why he got on with the guy. Nathan was surrounded by loud-mouthed and somewhat immature extroverts most of the day, and there was an above average share of prats and pranksters in the squad this year. Still, it made for a fun dressing room, even if did cross the boundary at times.

Nathan couldn't deny he was troubled by the increase in barbs involving 'homos' and 'paedos' since Byfield was arrested on the very first day back of training. Most of the guys had no objections to wearing rainbow laces when Stonewall came knocking once a year, but they couldn't see the correlation between supporting LGBT sportsmen and avoiding homophobic 'banter.'

Nathan was sure that if he were to ask the likes of Darren Petrie and Timo Bolz what their views were on gay athletes outside of the lad-centric sports dressing room, nothing but support would emanate from their mouths. But there was something about the group dynamics of all-male gatherings, that this foul-mouthed prejudice always came out. It was a hark-back to schooldays, but these were grown men, for fuck sake.

Nathan knew he had to address it, but somehow the right moment hadn't come. He didn't want it to take an incident of some sort, to bring matters to a head. What sort of incident, though? Timo Bolz was an interesting case, Nathan thought, not for the first time. There had been rumours circulating in the press for some time, now, that a couple of high profile Premier League players were gay but so far, these players had resisted all the potential financial incentives (how the world had changed) to become the first ever contemporary topflight player to come out the closet.

He was not a betting man, but if Nathan were to put money on it, his wager would be on Bolz. With his vain posturing in front of the dressing room mirror and that blonde quiff, Timo seemed far more concerned with his appearance than the rest of his team-mates put together. And then there was that limp-wristed gait as he showboated down the left wing, teasing the opposing right-back with his silky and vastly superior ball skills.

Fuck, I'm as bad as the rest of them, Nathan chastised himself inwardly. Just because the guy looked a bit 'poofy' didn't make him gay. For all they knew, Bolz could have a hareem full of Frauleins in his rented pad in Manchester. But somehow Nathan doubted it. A roomful of mirrors, more like!

Brooksy gave a small sigh and Nathan looked across, as his roommate for the evening turned onto his side, facing him now. Brooksy had kicked off the sheets, obviously hot, and lay there now, foetal, in just a pair of loose-fitting boxers. He didn't seem to have a blemish on his body, Nathan noted, the room partially lit up by a bluish moonlight. No godawful sleeve tattoos, not much body hair, either, by the looks of it, apart from his legs. He was curiously unspoilt somehow, Nathan thought. Not that he was in any way boyish in appearance, like Van Huizen or Huwsy ere - Brooksy had a square jaw and broad shoulders. He had fully developed, in a way that some of the younger players had not yet, but there was still something curiously pure about him. He appeared to have bypassed the usual sins of his gender and age, eschewing alcohol, girls and slovenly attitudes in favour of healthy pursuits and self-discipline. Maybe that was just a physio thing, Nathan thought to himself. But then again, you could never accuse Dennis Atkins of being overly concerned with his health and wellbeing, being perennially found outside with a fag in his mouth. Nathan winced at his own unintended pun. And Luisa was carrying some extra timber, though she had a kid that stayed at home with her partner. Kids porked you out, Nathan knew that from his sister - or at least that was Katrina's excuse for carrying around two stone extra.

Nathan turned his pillows and lay back, arms crossed behind his head, trying to zoom out. But somehow, confusing thoughts kept circling in his head, like mini vultures depriving him of his sleep that night. He was troubled, but he didn't want to give a name to his troubles. It was altogether easier to attribute his demons to the stresses and strains of being captain of a top football club and the constant media attention that attracted, exacerbated at present by the circus around the suicide of young Carey Hopkins. Now was not the time to open the lid on Pandora's box. Nathan lacked the self-awareness and broader life experience to know that the momentum of the inner contents pushing upwards could blast the lid off, despite a person's best efforts to keep the box firmly shut.

<h1 style="text-align:center">15</h1>

Sofia was a beautiful city, Brooksy thought, as he jogged along the broad, tree-lined boulevard away from the hotel at just before seven that Tuesday morning. He always noted how the space seemed somehow taller in Europe, the further south you travelled, unlike in the UK, where the clouds seemed to rest metres above your head.

It had taken him a good fifteen minutes to get out of bed that morning. Unusually for him, he had not slept too well, and he had not leapt out of bed and into action with his customary enthusiasm for the day ahead.

He'd nodded off soon enough, having been woken by a returning Nathan, but then he'd woken up again about three thirty and had only intermittently been able to doze off again before his alarm went off at 6.30. He knew Nathan had got up several times. Fuck, that guy was restless. Maybe that's why he had a room to himself - nobody else would tolerate his meanderings. The older man had seemed to get up and stare out the window several times, bathing the room in semi-light every time he flicked back the curtain to gaze out over Sofia skyline.

Nathan clearly had a lot on his mind, though Brooksy attributed this to the stresses of the job. Good job he's not the manager, or club owner, Brooksy thought to himself. He didn't expect anyone would want to be in the shoes of Owen French at the moment, though, with two paedos and a murdered schoolboy on his conscience.

Brooksy told himself he must be imagining things, but he had felt sure at certain points in the night, when he was trying desperately hard to fall back asleep, that Nathan had been staring at him. Brooksy shook his head, as he jogged around an old lady, laden with bags, struggling along the pavement in front of him. His mind had been playing tricks on him, influenced no doubt by the powerful driver of wishful thinking.

He was looking forward to his first match abroad with the team. Even if it was just a friendly, it was vital experience in his rapid ascent up the career ladder at North West Rangers. It was good having Luisa here, too. It took the pressure off somewhat, knowing an experienced physio was there to assist and advise.

♥♥♥♥♥

Nathan winced as he stood under the shower at 7.45 am that morning. He had a splitting headache, undoubtedly due to another night of poor sleep. He'd have to resort to pills at this rate. He knew OTC pills wouldn't affect any random drug tests, but he doubted those babies would do the trick, anyway.

He squirted some apple-scented shampoo and shower gel from the dispenser on the tiled wall and massaged it gently into his dark hair, lest he trigger another lightning bolt of pain.

"Morning, boss," Tango grunted, as Nathan joined him at the breakfast table ten minutes later. Tango was staring a large TV screen on the wall, which appeared to be tuned in to the Bulgarian equivalent of News 24.

"Didn't know your Bulgarian was up to it," Nathan commented, accepting a coffee gratefully from a young female waitress, who greeted the globally known footballer with a winning smile. He smiled back - that would make her day, he knew.

"They just had a sports report," Tango informed him. "Showed the other team training and then an interview with some police chappie. The concierge speaks good English, he told us they were reporting on crowd control for the match. Apparently they're laying on half the country's police force for the game. It's only a fucking friendly!"

"Not sure they do friendly, when it comes to British teams," Nathan commented dryly. It was troubling, all the same. Everyone knew of the horror stories associated with over-eager policing, when it came to British clubs in Europe. Many a fan had been incited to unplanned acts of violence by goading police officers and home fans, intent on causing trouble for away fans from the UK.

Sometimes the hostile atmosphere spilled onto the pitch, too, with racism from extreme sections of the creating a toxic atmosphere among the players of opposing teams. Nathan had seen many a player lose their head in such dark surroundings, despite their best intentions to stay cool in the pressure cooker of Eastern European football. Not that it was restricted to Eastern Europe, Nathan knew. He'd played in hostile environments in Italy, with the Ultras bellowing out their nasty vitriol, and Central Asia wasn't always a bed of roses either. In short, wherever there was dogma-driven politics or right-wing populism, there were racists and homophobes loudly in evidence.

Hopefully tonight would be different, Nathan thought, though somehow he doubted it.

"Did you sleep ok?" Tango asked, layering jam on a

toasted bagel.

Nathan grunted. "Nope."

"Brooksy a snorer?"

"Like you, you mean? No. Can't blame him, he slept like a baby. Just me. Can't fucking switch off, can I?"

"It'll get better," Tango reassured him. "It's a bleedin' circus at the moment, with all that's going on. Once the season starts properly, things will snap back into place, you'll see."

"I hope so," Nathan replied soberly. "Winning the shield might help. Give everyone a lift, at least."

"Yeah," Tango agreed. "Roll on Wembley on Sunday. Can't fucking wait."

"I reckon we stand a chance against City," Nathan replied, sipping at a milky coffee. "We could catch them unaware with the new boys. We've added speed to our technical skills now. That's what we were lacking last season. We were solid but unremarkable."

"Or is that just the two of us?" Tango laughed.

"Speak for yourself, Tango my lad," Nathan smiled. The headache was beginning to subside, thank God.

"Think the boss will play them all at once, then?" Tango enquired.

Nathan shook his head. "I reckon he'll start with Bolz on the left and Dazzer on the right and replace them with Huwsy and Sav in the second half. Reckon he might start with Van Huizen in midfield, though. He played a blinder in defensive midfield in training this week. He might be just a kid, but I reckon he's pretty mature as a player. Years ahead of Chas in his distribution. And I think he'll give Linda a runout in the second half, last twenty or so. Jordan's clearly our top striker, but Linda offers a bit of late pace in the game."

"A sort of early career Walcott, you mean?" Nathan nodded.

"Thank God the boss isn't into the whole friendly game substitute the whole fucking team thing," Tango remarked.

"Yeah, kills the game for everyone," Nathan agreed. The conversation on team tactics stopped as first team coach Johnny Ziegler joined them, tray laden with the healthier options on offer from the extensive breakfast buffet.

"These continental Europeans, put us all to shame," Tango commented, shoving a pain au chocolat into his mouth with all the decorum of a homeless man at a state a banquet.

"It's really not very hard, believe me," Ziegler replied dryly, neatly beheading his kiwi fruit. "You Brits are far closer to Americans than the rest of Europe with your dietary habits."

"Pah!" Aston Rideout snorted, joining them at the table. "What about you Krauts with your beer and jumbo sausages?"

Nathan nearly choked on his coffee.

"Never was a truer word said in jest, ay, Johnny?" Tango grinned.

Ziegler smiled conspiratorially and winked at the red-headed Scot. "We Krauts have nothing on these Scotsmen tossing their cabers."

Nathan laughed, smacking Tango on the back.

"Calling me a wanker, Johnny?" Tango laughed good-humouredly.

Nathan waved, as he saw Brooksy enter the room,

freshly showered, and obviously looking for somewhere to sit. He beckoned the physio over.

"Seen Luisa?" Brooksy asked casually, not wanting to look to keen to occupy the free space next to Ziegler and opposite Nathan.

"You won't see Luisa in here until the last minute," Nathan replied.

"Too busy with her beauty regime," Tango commented more than a mite sarcastically.

"Needs the whole hour," Rideout chipped in. Brooksy winced at the blatantly sexist barb. It was not as if Aston Rideout was much to look at, with his ridiculous Barclay style squared off fringe and gangling frame. And as for Mackay with his Ed Sheeran ginger facial fluff and potty mouth…

"Miaow!" Ziegler responded, grinning. Brooksy ignored them, out of loyalty for his colleague. He didn't think Luisa was as much of a minger as they made out, anyway. Sure she was a bit overweight and had a skin problem, but at least she wasn't a bitch or didn't get off her tits like most of the WAGS at North West - from what he had gathered so far from the first team chatgroup. He preferred her company to most of the lads on the team, whom, Nathan excepted, were pretty infantile. He supposed that was what came with having a relatively young squad, where the elder statesmen, such as Tango and Nathan, were themselves only in their mid to late twenties. Not that Tango could be described as mature, by any stretch of the imagination, Brooksy thought. He supposed Tango's happy-go-lucky piss-taking personality helped release some of the obvious strain Nathan was under.

"Join us, mate," Rideout encouraged Brooksy. 'We were just discussing the size of Johnny's sausage."

"How can I refuse such an invite?" Brooksy replied archly, but smiling at Nathan with his eyes.

Nathan looked away.

16

Tango Mackay was worried. Things weren't going too well out on the pitch. It had nothing to do with the home fans. True, there were enough police here to guard the whole fucking continent, not 18,000 locals at a low-key friendly game, but so far there had been no hint of the kind of racist abuse that had marred higher profile matches in the past few years.

It was Nathan that was bothering him. There was something not right with his defensive partner and friend. The semi-permanent scowl across the Englishman's face was nothing new, but it was more than that. There was something angry and unsettled about him, that seemed to have been building up ever since they'd returned to preseason training a few weeks back. His dark, secretive eyes, looking even more deeply set than ever.

Could Nathan's dark mood be solely attributed to the suicide of young Carey and the nasty business with Byfield and Atkins? Tango wasn't convinced. Awful though the whole affair was - and it was not yet proven that Carey's death was linked to the child sex abuse ring involving the two middle-aged men and/or Gregg Caine - it was not as if Nathan was personally implicated in any of it. In Tango's experience, unless you were Mother bloody Teresa, you didn't get that personally affected by events outside of you and your immediate family and circle of friends.

Perhaps Nathan was involved somehow? Tangofrowned, swigging from a bottle of water thrown on the pitch from Luisa, as play stopped for an injury on the Bulgarian team.

Could a younger Nathan have crossed swords with either of these guys in the past? Nathan was 27. It was certainly possible both geographically and timewise, but there was no way Nathan would elect to join a club which employed both of these men, if he'd suffered the kind of horrendous experiences outlined by Paul Stewart and David White and other footballers from the north-west of England.

But perhaps he'd been abused by someone else at another club, and this was bringing back bad memories? It would explain the anger and negativity Nathan exuded at the moment, Tango acknowledged to himself. He knew that the rest of the lads - and the footballing world in general - had him down as a rough diamond, the joker of the pack. But James Mackay did possess a softer, caring side, and he was genuinely concerned for his club and national teammate.

He watched as his tall teammate strode up the field to contest a drop ball with his opposite number. Nathan won it, but of course, and booted the ball upfield straight to the feet of Timo Bolz. The German crossed it inch perfect to the incoming Petter Lindstrom, who had started the second half after a clash of heads between Jordan Taylor and the Bulgarian keeper. Lindstrom brought it down off his chest and powered a volley into the top right corner of the net.

Tango whooped in delight and legged it upfield to join the throng of red shirts already gathered around the leggy Swede with his flowing blonde locks. It was his first oal for the team, outside of training.

Nathan, further up the field than Tango, walked

slowly up to Lindstrom and waited for the huddle to break. He patted 'Linda' on the back.

"Well done, mate, you took that beautifully."

That was praise indeed from the understated club captain and Lindstrom beamed. He would treasure that moment forever.

Tango forgot all about his earlier musings as a new energy filled the team, following Lindstrom's wonder strike. He cleared an easy ball from the opposition's winger up to Van Huizen in midfield and clapped appreciatively as the young Dutchman dummied it past two players and only just skimmed the post with a bending, swirling effort from the edge of the six yard post.

It could be a very exciting season, despite the inauspicious start.

♥♥♥♥♥

It wasn't too long, however, before Tango's misgivings returned. With just a quarter of an hour left of the match, Sporting Sofia's number two, a swarthy yob of a player, went scything into Nathan near the touchline. Nathan jumped over the incoming two-foot challenge, but the impetus sent him crashing into the hoardings. Dazed, it was only the quick thinking of several match officials that hauled him to safety before the home crowd got to him. The captain of North West Rangers and GB No 6 would be a valuable scalp for these thuggish ultras that had gathered near the touchline to voice their invective at the opposition.

Despite the cheers of the partisan crowd, the referee

was delivering a stern talking-to to the Bulgarian player, who did not try to protest his innocence. It was just a classic bit of lumpen showboating for the benefit of the crowd and testosterone-fuelled idiots the world over. Take out a global superstar and enjoy your fifteen minutes of ill-gained fame.

But the referee's admonishment was not enough for Nathan. He pushed the French referee away and started poking the short, squat Bulgarian no. 2 in the chest, yelling obscenities at him.

"You could have fucking killed me, you moron, what the fuck do you think you're doing?"

It wouldn't have taken an expert lipreader to work that one out from a distance.

Tango rushed over to separate Nathan from the opposition player. Nathan had entirely lost it and was on the brink of headbutting his opponent, when Tango and Petrie yanked him away.

"Pushing the referee is bad enough, headbutt this loser and you're in serious trouble," Tango remonstrated with Nathan, as he tried to escape from their grasp. The rest of the Bulgarian were now circling the referee, trying to get Nathan sent off. The referee was holding his hand to his ear, desperately trying to make out the instructions being yelled in his ear.

Finally, he pulled a red card out and Nathan was dismissed. Tango clapped the referee sardonically and a tiny bunch of Rangers supports broke out in a chant of 'The Referee's a Homer.'

Nathan stormed down the tunnel, head down, kicking a crate of energy drinks angrily en route.

"Ignore him," Dieter Jantzen commanded Ziegler,

ho made to follow Hunt. "I will talk to him later. He needs to calm down."

Brooksy watched the whole episode with horror. There was clearly more to this than some low-life journeyman from some shitty foreign team trying to get his pound of flesh from a star player. Nathan must come across this sort of stuff week in, week out, and had the battle scars to prove it.

"I need a pee," Brooksy shouted to Luisa's. The roar of the crowd was deafening, the home support galvanised by the sending off of Hunt. "There's only a little while left."

"No probs," Luisa replied, oblivious to Brooksy's concern for the North West captain.

Fortunately, the noise and general excitement around the stadium meant Brooksy could slip unnoticed past the North West bench into the tunnel.

He made his way to the away dressing room, where he found Nathan sat abjectly on the bench, head in hands, muddy socks and boots in a pile beside him.

"Mate," Brooksy said, sitting down beside him. "Just came to check you were ok."

He didn't feel it was quite his place to extend a brotherly arm around the club captain, so he just sat next to him for a moment.

Finally, Nathan raised his head. "Does the boss know you're here?"

Brooksy looked at him and felt his heart swell inside him as he saw there were tears in the older man's eyes.

"No," he replied. "I told Luisa I needed a pee."

"Best go have one then," Nathan sniffed.

Brooksy laughed and at that point, dared to put his

arm around Nathan."I lied."

But Nathan shook his arm off and stood up. He turned and faced Brooksy.

"You best be off. The team will be back in soon and the boss won't like it that you're here and not on the pitch where you should be."

"Hey, I just came to check…" Brooksy stood up, raising his palms in front of him in a gesture of 'woah, back off.'

"Thanks, but I'm fine," Nathan growled and took his shirt off. "I need a shower, so piss off back to the dugout."

Brooksy gave him a long hard look, then departed calmly, belying the angry hurt rising inside.

17

Nathan managed to bag a seat all to himself at the front of the plane on the return journey. It had been his choice and Jantzen had consented. In the end, he had escaped a bollocking from the firm but fair German. The Bulgarian lad had been asking for it all evening, in Jantzen and Ziegler's considered view, and Nathan was the biggest scalp of all for such vermin.

Besides, as Jantzen knew, it had been an incredibly difficult and stressful few weeks at the club, and Nathan had been involved, albeit indirectly, in much of the hoo-ha surrounding the arrests of Byfield and Atkins and the suicide of Carey Hopkins.

So, Nathan escaped with a warning, that if further any explosions of temper were witnessed in training that week, he, Jantzen, would not hesitate to drop him for the Community Shield final against City. That was enough to extract a promise from Nathan that he would be on his best behaviour from now on. Leading his team out at Wembley was every club captain's dream. Plus finals didn't come round too often, and this was only the second in the fledgling history of North West Rangers FC.

Fortunately, the rest of the team had the good sense to leave him alone on returning to the dressing room, following a hard-fought two one win over Sporting Sofia. Even Tango stopped short at a 'Alright, mate?' and directed his bonhomie at Dazzer and Rideout instead.

Nathan turned his phone to airplane mode as the small chartered plane prepared to take off, and put his headphones on to block out the noise of the plane and his teammates joshing in the rows behind him.

Several rows back, but in front of the majority of the first team, who were engaged in a rocky card game at the back of the plane, Brooksy sat next to Luisa. He stared
mostly out of the window, where the light was slowly fading, and tried to zone out of Luisa's incessant prattle about her kid.

What the fuck was wrong with Nathan? He wouldn't be the only one scratching their head and asking themselves that question, Brooksy was sure. He knew Jantzen had let him off with a minor warning, given the grisly tackle that had provoked the stormy reaction from Nathan, but it was hardly the first time - and wouldn't be the last - that a defender found themselves in a beefy scrap with an opposition player.

Brooksy was still smarting from Nathan throwing his arm off his shoulder and telling him to get the fuck out the dressing room, too. He had made Brooksy look like an out of step fool, and that hurt. Not that Brooksy would show it. He would keep his distance, sure, but he would not be off with Nathan. That wasn't his style, and it wasn't cool anyway, to react like a petulant kid in return.

"You know what I think?" Luisa said conspiratorially, inclining her head towards Brooksy.

Do I get a choice? Brooksy thought.

"I think he knew those men from another club - Nathan."

"So why join Rangers in the first place, then?" Brooksy replied distantly, pretending to look out the window, still. Luisa made a money gesture with her fingers and thumb.

"The money, honey," she stated, as he was not looking in her direction.

"Any top club would have offered big bucks for Hunt," Brooksy replied. "He had clubs from Italy and the Bundesliga after him. He wanted to join Rangers."

"Maybe then he…"

"Just stop right there, Luisa," Brooksy commanded, staring at her, warning lights in his blue eyes.

"I was going to say, maybe then he didn't know them after all."

Of course you were, Brooksy thought sarcastically to himself. He had seen another side to Luisa on this trip. While she was undoubtedly an adept and experienced physio, she was also an outrageous gossip, staying up until the late hours with Dazzer and Rideout and the other 'talkers' on the team.

It seemed many of the first team preferred his calmer, less talkative demeanour, particularly before a match, and Brooksy was beginning to come out of himself and assume a less subservient attitude towards the female physio.

♥♥♥♥♥

Thankfully, Alessandra had decided to stay at her own place late that Tuesday evening, when Nathan finally made it home. He really couldn't face any small talk, or even worse, her concern.

Nathan opened the fridge door, but he didn't feel hungry. His stomach was all churned up and he had a thumping headache. He grabbed a chilled water and swallowed some paracetamol instead, before heading upstairs for the sanctity of his super king-size divan.

Bet yet again, the demons of sleeplessness circled his throbbing head, not aided by the pounding rain outside, the humidity in the air finally finding a release.

Nathan wanted to cry, but the tears would not come this time. A message flashed up on his phone.

Here if you want to talk, but I won't ask again. Brooksy.

He'd been pretty rude to the guy, Nathan knew. But it was a bit fucking presumptuous, coming into the dressing room like that, even daring to put an arm around his shoulder. A junior physio who'd been at the club five minutes - who did he think he was?

Who do you think you are? A voice in Nathan's head said back to him. He flung the sheet off his naked body and walked to the window. He put his hands to his ears then yelled until his voice turned hoarse. It was going to be a long night.

18

It seemed that Greater Manchester Police had drawn a blank over the death of Carey Hopkins. No direct links could be found between Gregg Caine and the teenager. Whilst other members of the youth academy had come into contact with Caine - and were currently assisting police with further enquiries into Caine's activities both as a local football scout and PE teacher - there was nothing that linked Caine to Carey. Besides, in the words of one youth player, who had known of Caine's proclivities, Carey was not Gregg's type. It seemed Gregg Caine liked them dark and stocky, not ginger-haired and skinny.

Hopkins, unusually, had not owned a smartphone, but a trawl through his texts had revealed nothing out of the ordinary. There were certainly no signs of suicide ideation or desperate cries for help to friends. In fact, there was practically nothing on there, beyond a few messages to his parents and little brother. The phone, it appeared, had not been wiped.

An interview with Carey's parents revealed that he had recently lost an expensive iPhone they had saved up for, and justifiably angry, they had refused to replace it, insisting Carey used a cheap spare candy bar phone from home instead. Embarrassed to be seen with it, Carey had only used it on a needs-must basis, hence the relative low amounts of call activity on it. He did not own a laptop. The Hopkins family were not affluent. They had pinned their future hopes on their elder son's footballing talent and had been elated when Carey had signed for the Rangers Youth Academy, shortly after his sixteenth birthday last October. It was therefore a particularly devastating blow to lose him in such tragic circumstances. The mystery surrounding his suicide made it all the more painful to bear.

Whilst Jason and Susie Hopkins acknowledged that Carey had become somewhat withdrawn of late, they had found no particular reason to worry about him. They had attributed his low mood to teenage hormones and a suspicion that he was probably being teased by his teammates - he could be quite sensitive about his appearance. But they were sure it would settle down in a few weeks once the season started, because if there was one thing Carey had, it was a sweet left foot. Carey was almost guaranteed a place in the starting line-up, being the only natural left-sided player in the squad. The teasing would stop when the crosses came flying in from the wing, that was for sure. Football had certainly been his saving grace at school, which could be a cruel institution for red-haired freckled children of a sensitive disposition.

Neither could any trace of contact be found between Carey and the two men at the heart of recent historical child abuse allegations, Peter Byfield and Dennis Atkins. he 16 year old youth player simply would not have come into contact with either men and was too young to be implicated in any of the allegations made against them.

It had been decided not to subject the youth team to further questioning; they were already quite traumatised by the whole event. Instead, the boys were encouraged to contact the police or talk to their parents if they had any information, however trivial it might seem, that would assist the police in their investigation and help explain why Carey Hopkins chose to take his own life. As it was, the funeral was planned for next Thursday afternoon - a week tomorrow - and would be attended by the youth team, the academy staff and representatives from the Senior Squad, including Club Captain, Nathan Hunt and Vice Captain, James Mackay. The Hopkins were a Catholic family, it transpired, and the funeral would be held at Salford Cathedral to accommodate the large number of players and coaching staff, as well as former school friends, who would want to pay respects to the talented young footballer.

It was deemed better to get the funeral out of the way before the first team travelled down to London for the Community Shield a week Sunday. Black armbands would be worn in respect for Carey, and Jason and Susie Hopkins - along with younger son George - would be guests of honour at the match, provided they felt up to making the trip so shortly after laying their son to rest.

Reporters from the big rolling news stations, as well as journalists and photographers from local and national newspapers, were still camped outside both the Marchmont training ground and the Prosperity Stadium. It was a source of immense frustration to staff and players alike, who could barely step out their car without a barrage of questions being shouted across the barriers at them, no matter what time of day.

What was there to say, though? The dinosaurs had left the club and nobody knew why Carey Hopkins had killed himself.

Perhaps he should have just left Nathan alone after the sending off, Brooksy ruminated to himself, as he sat at home the next day. The players had a day off to recover from the match and travel and so he found himself at a loose end.

Well, not exactly - he had a tonne of personal admin to do, as the last few weeks had been something of a whirlwind. But Brooksy was too distracted to settle. He flicked the TV on aimlessly, but daytime television was just too awful to countenance, unless you liked buying knackered old houses or airing your dirty laundry in public. The news channels were marginally less obsessed with proceedings at Rangers, as a former member of the Royal Family was embroiled in a spat with the Daily Mail, but coverage would certainly resume in earnest with Carey's funeral on Thursday.

He picked up his phone for about the five hundredth time that day, but there was no message from Nathan. In fact, he'd had no contact with him since Nathan had made it clear he was not welcoming in the dressing room on Tuesday evening. He knew from the blue ticks that Nathan had received his message, which was a small comfort. At least Nathan knew he cared, even if he thought he was an arrogant prick or even worse, a total loser.

Brooksy's self-esteem was too strong to be down on himself for long. He had done what any decent person would do in the circumstances - he'd checked on a mate to see if they were alright. They had gone on a bike-ride together, they had shared a room. That made them at least acquaintances and possibly friends, by

Brooksy's reckoning, even if the friendship was at its very early stages.

Maybe Nathan had sensed that he was gay, and that was behind his rejection of him? Brooksy dismissed that idea. He'd done nothing to put that idea in Nathan's head and he was fairly sure, from feedback from friends and family, that he didn't give off 'gay vibes,' however one wanted to define them. Besides, he went out his way to avoid appearing 'poofy' in any way. It was not a good idea when he was working with male bodies as profession. Whilst Brooksy would never deliberately mislead or take a girlfriend for appearances' sake - that was just too cruel - he had no desire to make his life difficult by coming out in the heteronormative world of professional football. Maybe one day if he met someone special, that would be different. But for now, it was just not worth the hassle. Especially not when he'd just landed on his feet at one of the top clubs in the land, if not Europe.

Was he kidding himself that he could be mates with Nathan - given both their inequality of status within the Club and Brooksy's sexual attraction to him? But Nathan had invited him on a bike ride, Nathan had come to find him poolside at the hotel, and Nathan hadn't appeared to balk at the thought of sharing a room with him. There was nothing to suggest that the older man was against a friendship of sorts with him. He hadn't imagined it, had he - that fantastic evening at Lime Woods, where they had ridden through the forest and chatted as equals?

Brooksy felt confused. Was he on a hiding to nothing, trying to be friends with a straight guy to whom he had a well-disguised, but nevertheless intensely powerful, sexual attraction? And was it possible to be friends with Nathan, anyway? Only Tango had any semblance of a close relationship with Nathan at the club, but even Tango had known to stay well clear, both after the match in Sofia and on the plane ride home.

Was this just infatuation of a sort? Maybe it was pride, Brooksy thought. He deeply admired the aloof and self-contained older man, for his inner strength as much as his physical prowess. There was something about acquiring his respect and friendship that meant something to Brooksy.

He'd tried to explain it to his cousin in the States, for whom 'soccer' meant nothing. Heidi, who described herself as 'pansexual,' had never heard of Nathan Hunt and had just dismissed Brooksy's feelings as a ridiculous teenage crush that he needed to get over fast, at the risk of jeopardising his fledgling career.

"Everyone knows you don't make eyes at a het," Heidi had drawled, rolling her eyes at Brooksy on the Facetime call late the previous evening - her afternoon.

"What if he's not?" Brooksy had tried, pitifully.

"So he has a beautiful Italian girlfriend and he's a multi-millionaire, but secretly he has a crush on the club's junior physio, who happens to have a penis and live in a shithole in the middle of Manchester?" Heidi had scoffed.

"Well, when you put it like that…."

"Get over yourself, Nico!" Heidi had advised. Brooksy intended doing precisely that that morning. He slung his gym gear in a bag and headed for the local sports centre, nowhere near the Prosperity Stadium or

Nathan Hunt, to flog the hell out his body for a couple of hours.

19

Smashed it! Brooksy said aloud, consulting his list of things to do that he'd put together earlier that day. He never stayed downbeat or demotivated for long. He'd sorted a whole pile of niggly little admin jobs related to the move to Manchester and the new job at Rangers, caught up on laundry and even cleaned the kitchen. His 'shit-hole' as Heidi had put it was looking quite respectable. Brooksy had read somewhere recently that a famous footballer's wife - of Latin American extraction - had described Britain's second city as looking like the back of a fridge! He couldn't say Sheffield had been any better, to be honest, and London was pretty damn awful unless you lived in the leafy suburbs.

It was 9pm. He felt justified in finally enjoying some downtime. Brooksy changed into a white vest top and comfortable grey jersey shorts and flopped back on the sofa with a cup of tea.

He barely heard the intercom over the sound of Line of Duty and had to turn the volume down to be sure he wasn't hearing things. Who could it be at this time of night? He wasn't expecting a delivery and even the global online sweatshops didn't send out their delivery drivers this late. It was the intercom. He got up hastily.

"Yeah?"

"Is that Brooksy?" came a desperate sounding male voice.

"Nathan?" Brooksy queried, brow furrowed.

"Yeah… let me in."

Brooksy pressed the buzzer and waited for the

footsteps running up the stairs to arrive at his door.

He opened this door to a bedraggled Nathan Hunt, cycle helmet on head, rain dripping off his black anorak.

"You best come in," Brooksy stood aside to allow Nathan to enter his narrow hallway.

Nathan struggled to undo the clasp on his helmet, hands wet and cold from the rain.

"Come here," Brooksy said gently, and undid the clasp in an instant. He unzipped Nathan's jacket as the taller man just stood there shivering, droplets of water falling to the floor from his sodden clothes.

"Where did you leave your bike?" Brooksy asked, concerned. It was not a haven of security around these parts.

"I locked it to a pipe in the underground carpark," Nathan replied, teeth chattering.

"Should be ok, only residents go there," Brooksy commented. "How did you know where I lived?"

"I found a copy of your contract," Nathan replied.

"How the hell did you manage that?" Brooksy frowned. Weren't there some rules around GDPR? But it didn't matter for now.

"Look mate, I'm going to dig you out some dry clothes. They might be a bit short in the leg, but they'll do you for now. Wait here and I'll get you a towel, too."

Nathan just nodded gratefully and proceeded, with shaking fingers, to peel off his t-shirt and surf shorts, that were clinging to his wet thighs.

Brooksy reappeared with a thick fluffy bath towel, some lounge pants and an oversized t-shirt advertising popular brand of beer, that he'd won in a raffle.

"I'll leave you to get changed," Brooksy said

gently, placing the pile down on the sideboard. "The bathroom's on your right."

Nathan just nodded dejectedly and Brooksy respectfully left him to it. He returned to Vicky McClure et al and tried to digest what was happening in his hallway.

The guy was clearly in a right old state about something and hopefully Brooksy would be able to tease it out of him. Whatever it was, it was obviously eating Nathan up inside, to lead him to take the desperate measure of cycling five miles in this weather to reach out to the club physio that he barely knew.

Brooksy felt good inside - and justified - for having reached out to Nathan in his time of need and been trusted with his friendship. But he also felt deeply concerned. Whatever it was that was troubling Nathan, it was clearly not trivial. He didn't particularly care about the club or the final coming up - he hadn't been there long enough to feel a sense of loyalty yet. But he did care about Nathan Hunt. I love him, Brooksy acknowledged. There, he'd said it, if only to himself.

And just at that moment, Nathan entered the room, the loose fit lounge pants barely covering his calves, the t-shirt a snug fit. He looked curiously sexy, in the skin-tight t-shirt, hair all tousled, standing commando in the grey marl pants.

"Tea?" Brooksy asked.

Nathan nodded. "Just milk."

"Take a pew," Brooksy smiled and got up to make a brew.

"There you go," Brooksy said softly, placing the cup on the coffee table in front of Nathan a few minutes later.

Nathan just sat, head in his hands, as he had done in the dressing room that day.

"Are you going to tell me what's wrong?" Brooksy asked in the same gentle tone, moving the mug to one side and perching on the coffee table opposite Nathan.

Nathan just shook his head. "I can't," he replied, then promptly burst into loud racking sobs.

"Oh man," Brooksy exhaled and kneeling down between Nathan's akimbo legs, took the older man in his arms and held him tightly, stroking his tousled dark hair as he sobbed uncontrollably.

It was a good few minutes before Nathan pulled away, wiping his nose on the sleeve of his t-shirt.

"Here, drink this, it'll help," Brooksy said, handing Nathan his mug of tea.

"Thanks," Nathan replied hoarsely, sipping at the steaming beverage.

"You look absolutely exhausted," Brooksy commented, looking at him with grave concern.

"I haven't slept since… I can't remember when. And we have the final coming up on Sunday."

"Fuck the final, it's not important at the moment, mate. It's only the soddin' Community Shield. Nobody gives a shit about it."

"The club does and the fans do," Nathan replied. "We need to do it for Carey."

"I suppose so," Brooksy conceded. "But seriously mate, you've got to sort yourself out. You can't go on like this. Whatever it is that's eating you up, you've got to talk to someone."

"I just can't," Nathan reiterated, shaking his head. He brushed away the tears from his face, embarrassed. He took another sip of his tea, trying to regulate his breathing and stop more sobs from rising up.

He put the tea down and slapped the table. "Hell, I really don't need this at the moment. There's just too much going on at the club, I need to be strong!"

"You are strong, Nathan," Brooksy said quietly and soothingly. "But you'll be stronger when you address whatever it is that's keeping you awake at night."

"How did you get to be so fucking grown up?" Nathan frowned.

Brooksy shrugged, smiling inwardly. It was nice to have his maturity acknowledged by this guy he'd had on a pedestal for so long. So, Nathan did respect him and didn't see him as a stupid little upstart who dared infiltrate the first team dressing room.

"Good upbringing, I guess," he replied. "So, are you going to tell me what's going on?"

Nathan shook his head and looked Brooksy in the eye with bloodshot, moist eyes. "I just can't, ok?" His voice cracked again.

"Ow." Nathan clutched the side of his head.

"Do you have a headache?" Brooksy enquired.

"Permanently - for weeks. Like fucking lightning bolts in my head," Nathan muttered.

"Have you had it checked out?"

"I don't have a fucking brain tumour, if that's what you're driving at," Nathan raised his voice.

"Woah, back off!" Brooksy replied standing up, holding his hands out in front of him in a familiar gesture. "I was thinking more of concussion."

"I'm sorry…" Nathan said contritely, calming down.

"It's ok, mate," Brooksy replied more softly this

time. "Look - you need to rest. I'll get you some paracetamol. How about you sleep here tonight? You can have my bed; I'll kip on the sofa. I'll drive you back to your place in the morning - we can get your bike in the Golf, just about. It'll have to be early, though, or you'll be spotted leaving here. And I could do without the scandal!" Brooksy grinned but Nathan was not on his wavelength.

Nathan just nodded gratefully, cupping his tea in his hands. Brooksy disappeared to the bathroom to seek out some tablets, trying to quell the emotions swirling around inside. He desperately wanted to protect and care for this inspirational but troubled man, but it was not going to be easy. But how amazing, how bloody amazing, that he had sought refuge in Brooksy, of all people! Brooksy felt insanely privileged yet deeply concerned. It was a strange and heady combination of feelings. He handed Nathan a couple of paracetamol only (to be on the safe side) alongside a glass of water, then gathered some errant dishes from the living room and took them through to his tiny kitchen.

He should offer to make Nathan a sarnie or some toast or something. The guy probably hadn't eaten, judging by the state he was in. Maybe his girlfriend was out of town. They seemed to have a very casual relationship. She didn't even live with him permanently, from what Brooksy had heard - just flitted in and out of his house whenever she felt like it. It wasn't what he called a relationship. But then Brooksy knew he was quite old-fashioned in that respect. It came of being 'well brought-up', he laughed inwardly.

By the time Brooksy had returned from loading the

mini dishwasher, Nathan was curled up prostrate on the sofa, feet over the edge, fast asleep. Brooksy turned the television off and fetched a fleece blanket from the bedroom. He took a brief moment to take in Nathan's handsome bearded face. He resisted a strong temptation to plant a kiss on his cheek and an even stronger desire to trace a hand over his manhood, bulging out so obviously below the soft fabric of the loose fitting grey lounge pants, Brooksy covered him with the blanket. It was a hot evening, but Nathan had probably caught a chill, cycling all that way in the rain on zero sleep.

He turned the light off and retreated to his bedroom with the laptop. He could catch the rest of Kate Fleming and co. on iplayer, now that the TV was out of bounds. If he could concentrate.

20

Brooksy's eyes flickered open at just after one a.m., feeling a presence in his bedroom. He turned his head to see Nathan standing there, dressed only in the slightly comical mid-calf lounge pants, looking at him. There was something familiar about the image before him in the grey-black darkness.

"Nathan?"

"Can I lie next to you?" the older man mumbled. "I don't want to be alone."

"Uh… sure," Brooksy stuttered. He shifted over to a less central position on the bed and pulled the lightweight duvet back.

"Here, have a pillow." Brooksy extricated one from his pile of three and place it next to his. "Or did you want to go head to toe?"

Nathan just stared at him vacantly and got in beside Brooksy. He pulled the duvet over himself and closed his eyes.

Is he even fully awake? Brooksy wondered. Nathan appeared to be almost in a trance. He lay there still as a Mummy for several moments, listening to Nathan's breathing and wondering what to do. He remembered why the image of Nathan standing next to his bed had been familiar. Of course, the Sense Hotel in Sofia the other night. He'd felt somebody staring intently at him and had opened his eyes to see Nathan stood next to his bed, looking at him.

In the morning, Brooksy had told himself he'd been imagining things. But with hindsight, he'd been aware of a restless Nathan prowling around the hotel room, like a caged tiger. And Nathan had acknowledged earlier, that he hadn't slept for some time.

Brooksy really needed to pee. But he didn't want to wake Nathan, who appeared to have finally fallen asleep. Finally, his bladder won the argument, and he extricated himself from the duvet and tiptoed out to the bathroom.

Nathan had moved onto his back, by the time he returned. This time, Brooksy couldn't resist. He lay on his side taking in Nathan's body. He traced a finger down his lightly haired chest. Nathan did not even stir.

I love you, Brooksy whispered. There was no response. Sighing, Brooksy rolled over onto his back and closed his eyes. Nathan stirred this time, and rolled over, laying his head on Brooksy's bare chest, as if he'd done it a hundred times before.

Brooksy stopped breathing for a second. What the…. But once the initial surprise had subsided, Brooksy felt an overwhelming feeling of peace and wellbeing wash over him. He ruffled Nathan's curly dark hair and held him in his arms, stroking his shoulder and forearm.

I'll look after you, mate, he said quietly in the semi darkness. There was no reply.

♥♥♥♥♥

"I brought you a cup of tea," Brooksy said, just after 7 the following morning. He sat on the edge of the bed, next to Nathan, who was now spread-eagled on his front at an angle across the large divan. Brooksy placed it on the bedside table.

Nathan grunted then propped himself up on his

elbows, coming to. He turned his head to Brooksy, looking dazed and confused.

"You're at my house, mate," Brooksy said tenderly. "Remember?"

"Hmph," Nathan grunted and pulled himself up to a sitting position on the edge of the bed.

"You couldn't sleep," Brooksy reminded him, as Nathan appeared to be confused as to why he was in the bedroom of the first team physio.

"What's the time?" he mumbled.

"Just after seven," Brooksy replied. "Do you want breakfast?"

Nathan just shook his head.

"I dried your clothes in the laundry downstairs. I got up early," Brooksy informed him. That statement was not strictly true; Brooksy had been unable to sleep with both the bulk and sensation of Nathan snuggled up to him, and had given up the ghost by 5.30 am.

But Nathan just ignored him, cupping his tea in his hands and staring into space.

Thanks, Brooksy, that was nice of you, Brooksy thought ironically to himself, leaving the bedroom to give Nathan space.

♥♥♥♥♥

Nathan sat in silence all the way to his house, his bike squidged into the back of Brooksy's blue Golf, alongside both of their training gear. His dark presence seemed to fill the whole car, Brooksy thought, as he carefully negotiated the rush-hour traffic in Manchester that Thursday morning.

Nathan was fiddling with his phone, though Brooksy sensed it was a ploy to avoid communication. He had barely said a word since Brooksy had woken him with a cup of tea earlier that morning. The invention of the smartphone must have come as such a tonic for the socially challenged, Brooksy thought to himself.

"We're going to be a bit late for training," Brooksy informed him, as they finally hit the road out of town towards Nathan's luxury pad in Westvale.

"We'll go separately. You go before me," Nathan finally spoke. "I need to have breakfast." He had already showered at Brooksy's but had not felt hungry at 7.30 am.

"You shouldn't drive," Brooksy said seriously.

"I'll get Annie to take me," Nathan replied curtly, referring to his agent.

"What about your girlfriend?" Brooksy asked.

"She's out of town. And she's not my girlfriend," Nathan stated matter-of-factly, dialling Annie Wells, his agent.

"She's just for cuddles?" Brooksy enquired, trying to sound jokey but failing dismally. "Or appearances?" He cast a sidelong look at Nathan, who felt his eyes on him this time.

"Fuck off, Brooksy," Nathan replied and waited for Annie to pick up.

Brooksy checked the rear-view mirror. He had a pretty strong sense now what was eating away at Nathan Hunt, as he sat in the driver's seat.

21

Brooksy had fully anticipated that Nathan would blank him for the next few days. Had he been a betting man, he would have put money on it. Now that Brooksy had seen Nathan at his most vulnerable, it followed suit that the reticent and proud Nathan would keep his distance, undoubtedly mortified that he had let his guard slip.

But Brooksy knew that he just needed to bide his time. He was convinced only Alessandra at most knew of Nathan's secret, besides himself. And Nathan had shown that he needed Brooksy's support, even if he had to be at his absolute lowest to ask for help.

Brooksy mulled over Nathan's relationship with the Italian woman, as he cleaned down the surfaces in the physio room. What was in it for her? She was successful in her own right, and certainly didn't need to be seen on the arm of a famous footballer to earn her kudos. Nathan had just said she wasn't his girlfriend - not that they didn't have a sexual relationship of any kind. Maybe he was bisexual. Maybe she was, for that matter. Maybe she just scratched an itch for him, but he preferred men. Or perhaps Brooksy had misread the whole thing, and he was just depressed and in need of some human comfort. Nah! Brooksy dismissed that thought almost as soon as it landed in his head. Men did not cuddle up to each other in bed if they were straight. It just didn't happen, at least not in his experience of straight men. There was too much at stake, particularly in the macho world of football, one of the last bastions of rampant heteronormativity in the UK.

Or perhaps Nathan and Alessandra Esposito really were just friends, but allowed everyone to think otherwise, for the sake of convenience. That felt the most plausible explanation to Brooksy, the one that resonated in both his head and his gut. He couldn't imagine Alessandra would be able to bear this state of affairs, if she was actually in love with Nathan.

He had heard other players comment about the relative lack of commitment in their relationship, compared to say Tango and Eilidh or Aston Rideout and his doting wife, Kelly.

A friendship with social benefits made the most sense and accounted for the fact that Alessandra had her own property in the middle of town, where she appeared to spend the majority of her time.

"Got room for a little one?" Rideout popped his head round the door.

"Ha ha," Brooksy laughed. Rideout was 6' 5 in height, even taller than Nathan.

"What can I do for you?"

"Johnny sent me across. Got a slight calf strain, nothing major."

"I know, I know, you want me to tell Johnny it's nothing much and of course you can play in the final?"

"You got it, kiddo," Rideout laughed and sat on the bench.

"How's training today?" Brooksy enquired, washing his hands in preparation.

"Fine. New lads blending in well - well, you saw how well they did the other night. Nathan's still a grumpy sod. Don't know what's wrong with him at the moment. He's been like that since we came back. Not sure why.

Maybe he's had a bust up with that tasty bird of his. You know he went on holiday lone when the season ended? Strange guy."

"No, I didn't," Brooksy replied, feigning nonchalance.

"Went to fucking Mexico all on his tod for three weeks!"

Brooksy had realised fairly early on that Rideout was the chief gossip in the team. He and Luisa could give each other a run for their money, Brooksy thought.

He shrugged, massaging oil into Rideout's skinny calves. "Maybe he has family out there."

"Nah! He's just a loner. Either that, or he's got some secret señorita stowed away in Buenos Aires!"

"That's in Argentina," Brooksy corrected him. "I guess nobody recognises him over there - not like if he went on holiday in Europe."

"Bit excessive though, isn't it?" Rideout commented. "I mean, who goes to the other side of the world on their friggin' own for the summer?"

Someone who wants to get away from it all and live a different life for a few weeks, Brooksy thought to himself. There were lots of hot men in Central and South America, he'd heard from his cousin, and gay sex was in plentiful abundance, especially in the big cities.

Just at that point, Johnny Ziegler appeared in the open doorway.

"Brooksy, can I have a word when you're done? I'll be in my room."

Aston whistled. "Who's been a naughty boy then?"

Brooksy looked perplexed. "I don't know what he wants."

But Brooksy hadn't done anything wrong, as he found

out ten minutes later, sat opposite Ziegler in the unfamiliar surroundings of his office. He sensed Ziegler wasn't over familiar with his office, either, as some of the furniture therein still smelt new.

"Thanks for coming," Ziegler said seriously, getting up to shut the door behind Brooksy, to give them privacy. "Don't worry," he added, sensing Brooksy's discomfort. You haven't done anything wrong - far from it, the boys are raving about you."

"That's good to hear," Brooksy smiled nervously. "So, what can I do for you?" he added, a little more confidently.

Ziegler intertwined his figures before him on the desk. "It's about Nathan. We're worried about him."

"We?" Brooksy queried.

"Tango and the boss. We thought he might have said something to you. You shared a room the other night and seem quite friendly."

Brooksy shrugged. "It was just an error at the hotel."

"I know that," Ziegler replied. "But we thought he might have said something that gave you a clue why he's been like a bear with a sore head."

Ziegler liked his English idioms, Brooksy had noted.

Brooksy shrugged again. "He barely said a word, to be honest, boss."

"But did you overhear him - on the phone to his girlfriend maybe?"

She's not his girlfriend, Brooksy wanted to say, but it was not his secret to tell.

He shook his head instead. "I hardly saw him. He was up late, chatting to the new boys. I went to bed early; I was tired from the travelling and wanted to be alert for the game."

Ziegler sighed leaning back in his chair. He looked Brooksy directly in the eye. Could he trust the young lad? From all the conversations he'd had with the first team, the physio was a welcome breath of mature fresh air compared to the verbally incontinent Luisa de Sousa.

"The thing is, Brooksy," Ziegler said eventually. "Nathan wasn't up late chatting to the new players, he disappeared off somewhere and nobody knows where."

Brooksy took in this new information.

"I suspect he just went off for a walk, to be alone," he replied evenly after a moment. "I've noticed he needs his space. Doesn't even get in the lift with everyone else. Probably waited until it was dark, so that nobody would recognise him."

Ziegler frowned, drumming his fingers on the table. "You were all told not to leave the hotel."

"Have you spoken to him?" Brooksy asked.

Ziegler shook his head. "Not yet. It's all a bit sensitive. We were wondering if you knew anything? I'm sure you're aware from the match the other night, he's not quite been himself lately."

"I don't really feel I've been here long enough to know what he's really like, to be honest, boss," Brooksy replied. "He'd be more likely to confide in Tango."

Ziegler shook his head again. "Tango says Nathan hasn't had a proper conversation with him in weeks. He's been really distant."

He stared at Brooksy, which made the younger man feel distinctly uncomfortable.

"So, you have no idea what's wrong with him?"

Brooksy shook his head. Time to bat it back. "What are your thoughts?"

Ziegler took a minute to reply, weighing up the risks again. He took the plunge.

"Dieter and I are worried this … this bad mood of his… has kicked off with the child abuse allegations. We're worried he has had some bad experiences in the past and this has dragged it all up. We don't think he had any links with Peter Byfield or Dennis Atkins, or why else would he join Rangers, knowing they were there?"

Brooksy considered this viewpoint. He had to admit, the thought had also crossed his mind, and it might account for why Nathan had sought comfort but not sex. Perhaps he had entirely misread the situation. Perhaps Nathan was straight, but just couldn't hack a full-on relationship with anyone, owing to shit that had happened in his past. He'd read about the depression and loneliness caused by childhood abuse in the memoirs of some of the top players sickeningly targeted by child sex abusers in the world of football. It would explain why Nathan seemed permanently morose and detached. Had he let wishful thinking colour his judgement? There was certainly nothing outwardly gay about Nathan Hunt. Brooksy's gaydar had not been sounding at any stage in his dealings with Nathan - until Nathan had cuddled up to him in bed last night. But then again, Nathan had been half-asleep. Brooksy felt perplexed now, the earlier inward euphoria fast dissolving.

Ziegler sighed yet again. "Ok, Brooksy, if you don't know anything either, then we will have to talk to him. We didn't have this conversation, ok?"

"Of course, boss," Brooksy replied quietly. "I won't

say a word to anyone. Not that anyone ever asks my opinion about anything. They just talk at me."

Johnny smiled this time. "Like our very shy goalkeeper?"

Brooksy groaned. "He could talk all four legs off a donkey, boss." Ziegler would appreciate that. Like many foreign coaches who had done intensive English language training, he loved his English idioms!

Ziegler laughed out loud. He did.

22

Nathan had to admit, he'd thought it was overkill when the club had arranged for Salford Cathedral to host Carey Hopkins' funeral.

But sitting in the second row inside the impressive edifice, he had to acknowledge that it had been a good call. The building was rapidly filling up with a mixture of shell-shocked family members, former schools pupils, club dignitaries and the full youth academy team, under a three line whip to dress smartly in suits and club ties. They brushed up pretty well, the majority of them, Nathan thought. Just a few Luca Vialli giant tie knots and bed-head greasy bonces.

He was the sole representative from the first team, and had been given a ringside seat alongside Club Director Owen French and Club Owner, Juan-Pedro Morales. It had been a blessed relief to escape the media scrum outside for the calming sanctity of the huge Catholic cathedral.

Nathan was not a religious man, but he had to admit, there was something impressive about the still beauty of this inner sanctum. He could appreciate that this might be a place where a man could find at least temporary relief for his troubled soul. Perhaps he should check it out sometime, when it wasn't so busy.

"He had a huge family," French commented.

"Catholic, wasn't he," Morales replied matter-of-factly.

Nathan wasn't sure that these stereotypes still held sway. He had known plenty Catholic families, growing up and plying his trade in and around Liverpool, and by and large, they mostly had the same number of kids as everyone else - or at least they did in the middle-class environment he had called home. Nathan stood up straight and faced forward, as the music signalled the arrival of the funeral party.

He felt a lump form in his throat as six Youth Academy players, dressed in the first team kit, carried the coffin to the front, bedecked in the red and blue team flag. Despite selecting the most developed lads from the team, they still seemed so small and so young to Nathan.

Poor kids, French commented, seeing the tears streaming down the cheeks of at least two of the pallbearers. Nathan noted that Morales himself was in floods. It was a tragic day for all concerned.

"Family, friends, footballers," the presiding priest began. He's been practising that, Nathan thought cynically to himself. "We are gathered here to celebrate the life - so tragically cut short - of Carey Hopkins."

He's definitely showing off for the big screen outside Nathan thought uncharitably. And why does he have to have a fucking dress on?

He took his notes out of his pocket and briefly read through them. As Carey's idol, he had been asked to give a brief reading - from Carey's own journal, of all places. At least it wasn't a Bible passage. He was used to speaking in front of the public, but even so, he would have struggled with a Bible reading or prayer of any sort. It was a good job he was pretty stoic though - this highly personal journal entry, penned by an overawed Carey on signing youth academy terms with the Club, was enough to reduce anyone to tears.

And indeed it did, some twenty minutes in, when

Nathan delivered it from the pulpit, following the priest's address. It was the clip that would feature heavily on both regional and national news later that evening, alongside the young pallbearers and a teary address from Carey's uncle, Paul Hopkins - and of course, the mandatory discussion item on male mental health. It was noted that, interestingly, Carey had stopped writing his journal just a few weeks later, as if the young lad had run out of positive thoughts - or at least that was the spin the press were putting on it. Maybe he'd just run out of time, or grown out of it, Nathan thought. It was a kind of teenage thing to do, like writing poetry or something - not that he'd ever done either. That would have been entirely out of character, to give his inner thought life the time of day, let alone consign it to posterity in the form of a journal or creative effort.

As the mourners began to spill out of the Cathedral nearly forty minutes later, Nathan took the opportunity to nip to the loo. It would be sometime before those in the front row - outside of the direct family - would be able to leave the building.

He was just leaving the Gents when he was tentatively approached by a young lad he vaguely recognised from the Youth Academy.

"Nathan, you don't know me, but I wondered if I could have a quick word?"

He was well-spoken for an academy lad, Nathan noted. Then he remembered - he was Owen French's nephew, wasn't he? He'd got slated by the other lads, who'd accused French of nepotism for giving Charlie Wolfson a contract. It was fair to say, Wolfson was not exactly gifted in the technical skills department, though he was a solid enough defensive midfielder.

"Sure," Nathan replied. "It'll be a while until we get out of here."

Charlie shuffled nervously. "It's kind of private."

"Ok…" Nathan looked around him. He put a guiding hand on the teenager's back and steered him beyond the lavatories to a side room further down the corridor, where the priest had spoken to those involved in the service prior to its starting. He shut the door behind them.

"What's up?"

The lad was clearly distraught. Nathan handed him a clean handkerchief from his pocket as the lad dissolved into tears.

"I'm sorry, so sorry," he apologised through his tears.

"Please, don't worry," Nathan batted him away. "It's a tough day for all of us."

"It's not that… well, it is… but there's something else."

Nathan pulled out a chair for them both and indicated that Charlie should sit down. He waited for the lad to compose himself.

"I know we were supposed to tell the police anything we knew, but…"

"But?" Nathan probed, feeling his heart skip a beat.

"But I promised Carey I wouldn't say a word, and…"

"You want to respect his memory," Nathan completed his sentence. Charlie nodded miserably.

"But his family need to understand what's happened, so that they can achieve some semblance of peace," Nathan stated.

"I know…" Charlie sniffed.

"So it's kind of a duty, if you know anything relevant," Nathan reminded him. "I'm not a parent - yet – but I know if I was his dad, I'd want to have some answers."

Charlie broke into more sobs.

"It is to do with the child abuse stuff, about that teacher?" Nathan asked gently.

Charlie shook his head. "He never had anything to do with him. Or those two old guys, either."

Nathan paused to digest this information. That corroborated police reports, that they had found no link between Hopkins' suicide and the unsavoury antics of Caine, Byfield or Atkins.

"Was he being teased?" Nathan persevered. "I don't mean to be unkind, but he was a bit of a funny looking kid."

He remembered a conversation he'd once had with his sister's partner, a GP in the North East. Apparently that was how doctors referred internally in shorthand to some kids in their practice - FLKs - funny looking kids.

"No… yes…"

"Charlie?"

Charlie looked up at Nathan, wiping the tears away. "I mean yes, he was being teased, but not about being ginger and that."

"And it was nothing to do with Gregg Caine and the allegations about him?"

Charlie shook his head vehemently. "I told you, Carey didn't have anything to do with him. He knew who he was sure, cos he was an ex pupil, but Gregg was never interested in him. He was totally clueless about what was going on."

"So?"

Charlie took a deep breath then looked Nathan square in the eye. "Carey was gay."

Nathan took a moment. "He told you that?"

Charlie nodded, twisting the wet handkerchief in his hands.

"Did you tell anyone?" he asked gently, almost certain what the answer would be. Charlie indicated his head, miserably.

"Who did you tell, Charlie?"

"I lost my temper with him - he could be an irritating little wanker at times…"

"Can't we all?" Nathan smiled ruefully.

"He'd been winding me up all morning… this was about a month ago… telling me I'd only got on the team cos my Uncle's the Director. That I was shit, that I wouldn't even cut it in the Under 14s… I feel bad saying this."

"Don't worry about that, Charlie," Nathan comforted him. "He wasn't a saint, nobody is, I get that. It's not speaking ill of the dead, it's just being truthful."

Charlie looked at him gratefully.

"So about a month ago, he'd been winding you up in training," Nathan surmised, encouraging the seventeen year old to continue with his account.

Charlie nodded. "We were on the same team in training and I lost a possession a few times, and over hit a few passes to him. He kept telling me I was a waste of space on the pitch, in front of everyone."

"That's not cool," Nathan frowned.

"He was like that," Charlie stated. "I know it was

because he was insecure, because people teased him for being skinny and ginger and that. He, like, tried to compensate by flexing about his skills where he could. Well, me, mainly," he conceded. "I'm the weakest link on the team."

Nathan felt for him. It obviously had its disadvantages as well, being the nephew of the Club Director. "So, then?"

"So it continued in the dressing room. He was calling me names, like faggot and spaz and stuff."

"And you lost it, because of the hypocrisy of it?" Charlie nodded miserably. "I shouted out in front of everyone, you're the fucking faggot, Hoppy. We all know where your phone got to. Your dad smashed it up when he read your Instagram, you fucking homo."

Charlie shook his head. "I'm so ashamed of myself." Nathan shook his head, squeezing the young man's wrist. "Mate, many lads would have done the same thing in the circumstances. I'm not justifying outing him, but he'd been winding you up and deflecting from himself by calling you gay."

Charlie nodded. "That's it."

"So that's what happened to his phone…" Nathan wondered out loud. "His dad told the police Carey had lost it and they couldn't afford to buy him a new one. That's why he had that crappy Nokia job."

Charlie shook his head. "His dad stamped on it then smashed it with a hammer. He had his suspicions about Carey and looked at his phone. Found some dating app thing on it and a load of pictures of guys on Instagram or Snapchat or something. Went fucking mental."

"And Carey told you this?" Nathan checked.

Charlie nodded. "He was late for training one week, and had obviously been crying. He got a bollocking from the coach, of course, which made it worse. I asked him why he was late, and he told me he'd had an argument with his dad."

"And then he told you he was gay?"

"He told me a few days later, on a training run," Charlie sniffed. "I feel so shit. He trusted me with that, and I let him down."

"It was shit," Nathan agreed, never one to mince words, "but I understand how it happened, and I don't think you reacted any differently from how most lads would, in the circumstances. It's tough out there at times, trust me, I know it. Teenage lads can be cruel, and so can grown lads for that matter. Sometimes the banter goes too far."

"It does," Charlie agreed.

"It's no different with the first team, Charlie," Nathan informed him, soberly. "It's Fucking Homo this, Fucking Paedo that, at the moment. I try to address it, but it's hard. Cos then they turn on you, and sometimes you could just do without the grief. There's enough to think bout without inviting that sort of aggro. But you have to be man enough to stick to your principles. It comes with age, well, for most people - but even I'm struggling with that at the moment."

"Yeah, I can imagine, with all that's happened lately," Charlie nodded slowly, appreciating the honesty of the Club Captain.

"So that's why Carey slashed…err, too his own life?" Nathan doublechecked.

Charlie nodded. "After I said all that stuff in the

dressing room, he was just teased constantly. The lads banned him from the showers. That's why he killed himself in the shower. To make a point, I guess."

Nathan nodded slowly. It all made horrible sense, now. "You did right to tell me, Charlie," he reassured the lad. "Look me in the eye."

Charlie looked up.

"You did the right thing."

Charlie nodded. "Thank you.… What will you do, now?"

"I need to talk to the police," Nathan replied. "And maybe they'll let me talk to the parents, or at least his Dad."

"About the sexuality stuff?"

"Yes."

23

The police had allowed Nathan to accompany them to the Hopkins' family home later that evening. They had taken a statement from Charlie Wolfson, and Owen French had been informed of his nephew's indirect role in the suicide of Carey Hopkins. French had been visibly upset by the revelation. Nathan had a feeling that the club culture around sexuality and what constituted banter was about to change. If there were any positives to come out of this whole tragic incident, then that was surely one of them.

Jason Hopkins, already in pieces, had unravelled entirely when Nathan explained to him what had happened. Nathan now knew why Hopkins Senior had sat head in his hands throughout the service in the Cathedral. He was clearly consumed with guilt.

In the circumstances, the police had refrained from charging Jason Hopkins with withholding vital evidence, on the subject of Carey's iPhone and sexuality. His wife was clearly not so forgiving. Carey's sexuality had already appeared to have created a major rift between them, leading to arguments in the night that had further added to Carey's misery. It was perhaps obvious why mothers of gay sons found it altogether easier to deal with than the fathers did, but all the same, it was a terrible thing to reject your child in that way, for something they could not do a blind thing about. They said UK culture was changing, but Nathan saw little evidence of it when it came to male homosexuality in particular, especially in the macho working-class world of football. They couldn't even get a footballer to make documentaries about homophobia, getting that retired Welsh rugby fella to do the honours instead.

Nathan was not convinced that marriage was going to survive. It was the kid brother he felt sorry for. Who would want to be an innocent bystander in that household?

There were precious few innocent bystanders in such cases, Nathan thought soberly. He was as guilty as the rest of them. Sins of omission were every bit as bad as sins of commission. What little experience he had of church in his youth had at least impressed that on him. What you neglected to do and say, when you ought to speak up, was every bit as bad as what the likes of Charlie Wolfson or Jason Hopkins had done to Carey. What was that phrase they'd been given in that equality training they'd all had last year? The standard you walk past is the standard you accept. Yes, that was it. Apparently, some ex-army guy from Oz had once said that. And he, Nathan Hunt, was a coward of the highest order, too. The dressing room culture would have to change, lest another tragedy like this happened. That was the sermon he would have preached, had he been a priest in full possession of the facts earlier that day.

At least they could draw a line under the event itself, and focus on the upcoming final at Wembley, Nathan thought, as he drove his Jeep along the ring road out of Manchester towards Westvale.

Rumour had it that City were planning on resting a few of their key players, in preparation for the start of the British Premier League. If that was true, then it was pretty disrespectful of the Community Shield and all the charities that benefitted from the revenues it raised. But

Nathan wouldn't have put it past City to be playing mind games. It wouldn't have been the first time that a top team had spun such a yarn before a final.

Nathan started to plan a rousing team talk in his head - on how best to honour the memory of tragic Carey Hopkins.

24

Sunday 4th August was disappointingly cloudy, following a week bathed in sunshine. You wanted one or the other at Wembley, Nathan thought, as he disembarked the plane that morning - either sunshine, or failing that, rain, so that the roof would be pulled across, creating that amazing, intense atmosphere among the rival fans and players.

He'd got his speech done too, mercifully allowed to sit alone once more on board the plane making the short hop from Manchester to London.

Brooksy and the rest of the squad had noted that Nathan appeared to have perked up a bit. Nobody beyond French, Morales and Dieter Jantzen had been informed as yet of the motive for Carey Hopkins' suicide. Nathan had been waiting for permission from the police and grieving parents to say his piece. Permission had now been granted.

"I don't need to tell you - but I will anyway - of how much winning this final would mean to the family and friends of Carey Hopkins," Nathan underlined to the team, handing out the black armbands.

"Losing this game is simply not an option. And I don't want to see anyone sitting back and parking the bus if we get an early goal." He looked around the dressing room, commanding the total respect of every member of the squad. Even Bolz and Petrie were silent.

"We have some amazing attacking options in the team at the moment. The boss has picked an attacking formation and he expects to see us get at them from the off. Is that clear?"

"Heil Hunt!" Petrie saluted his captain.

"Fuck off, Dazzer," Nathan grinned, breaking the tension. The rest of the talk could wait until later. He needed them pumped up and positive for now.

♥♥♥♥♥

Defending a one nil lead was not an option, as it transpired. It had indeed been a ruse - City had put out a full-strength squad and had cruised to a comfortable two il lead by halftime.

It seemed the Rangers boys had been emotionally affected by a weeping Jason and Susie Hopkins being introduced to the fans before the match and presented with a red and blue wreath by Owen French and Juan-Pedro Morales on behalf of the club. A picture of a freckle-faced Carey Hopkins, beaming with pride, was put up on the big screens at either end, and a minute's applause - impeccably observed - held in memory of the talented yet tragic youth academy player.

It was up to Nathan to lift their spirits. The timing of the tribute was not ideal from a preparational perspective, but it could hardly have been held at halftime or after the match, Nathan conceded.

He allowed the players to visit the bathroom and grab a water before gathering them in a huddle to highlight once more the necessity of winning the match. They had the players to overwrite a two goal deficit and City had shown signs already of taking their foot off the gas, making several strategic substitutions, clearly with the season's starter against Glasgow Celtic in mind.

Nathan intended to lead from the front, and seemed to

find an extra foot in the air as he leapt up to clear a ball with his head within seconds of the restart. He noted with relief that his team talk had appeared to lift the players and give them a new lease of life, as Dazzer bombed down the right wing with a turbo charge in his feet. He danced past three City players, before whipping the ball into the box. It was a battle between Lindstrom and Taylor as to who would get there first. Lindstrom won and poked the ball beyond the outrushing City goalkeeper with the edge of his blue boot.

The red and blue end of the Stadium rose to their feet with a thundering yell of appreciation as "Linda" ran to the hoardings, a gleeful Jordan Taylor in hot pursuit.

Lindstrom cupped his hands to his ears, and did a little mincing walk with a handbag, with reference to the frequent teasing aimed at him on account of his rather feminine appearance. Nathan groaned, despite his euphoria, as he jogged down the pitch to join the relieved celebrations. It was going to be no small job, getting this bunch to ditch the prejudice.

The team were flying, now. As Nathan slid into City's no. 7, mercifully outside the box, for which he earned a yellow card, a familiar chant rose up among the 40,000 Rangers fans, to the tune of the Shamen's 90s dance classic, Ebineezer Goode: *He's a cunt, he's a cunt, he's Nathan Hunt. He's a cunt, he's a cunt...*

Nathan grinned. It was crass and his mum didn't approve, but it always made him feel good. It appealed to his tough guy image.

Within the space of five minutes, Rangers had caught City unaware again with their speed demons, this time on the right wing. Bolz shimmied past two defenders across the box before rocketing a swerving volley into the top corner, catching the keeper entirely unawares.

The stadium erupted again in a sea of red and blue waving flags and bare-chested Mancunians. This time, Bolz did not celebrate, but sped back to the half-way line, ball in hand, gesturing with his arms for the crowd to keep the noise up.

This is Roy of the Rovers stuff! An excitable radio commentator yelled into his microphone, several rows above where Brooksy was stationed with Luisa, kitbags at the ready. *Or should that be Roy of the Rangers?*

Brooksy groaned at the pun from his position on the bench. It was two all, with half an hour to go now. The game would go straight to penalties if this remained the score at full time, the extra time option having been abandoned some years ago. It certainly raised the stakes and enjoyment factor for the crowd, Brooksy knew. It got kind of tedious watching players limping around with cramp in extra time, all so terrified of conceding, that they rarely threatened the opposition's goal.

Brooksy rose to his feet fifteen minutes later as Bolz was fouled on the edge of the box by a particularly tasty tackle by the City wingback.

The Rangers section of the crowd bayed for a penalty, and there was an agonising wait as the referee consulted with the linesman for what seemed like an age, then was beckoned over to the screen pitch side. Finally the referee shook his head and called a freekick instead.

Nathan, shielding his eyes from the sun, which had just decided to show its face at long last, began his ascent up the pitch from box to box, as a freekick was confirmed. A specialist at banging the ball in the net with his forehead at set pieces, there was no way he was going to avoid a punt on this one, in the last fifteen minutes of the game. Captain Fantastic Hunt jogs to the box, fancying his chance to win it for Rangers, the deeply unoriginal amateur yelled down his mike.

Jockeying for position in the cramped six-yard box, Nathan rose to the occasion as a fully-recovered Bolz lofted the ball high over the City wall. Finding an extra spring in his legs and avoiding pushing down on the City defender and conceding a foul, Nathan leapt upwards, a good six inches above his nearest rival. He dipped forward and launched the centre of his forehead at the ball and with a gratifying thump, it cannoned off his head and over the outstretched hands of the City no.1 and into the top corner.

Pandemonium broke out as Nathan ran to the side of the pitch, held his arms aloft and closed his eyes, head tilted heavenwards. The noise was thunderous as his team-mates circled him, raising him aloft. Brooksy and Luisa on the touchline, lost all control and joined the throng around him. Even Nathan had a broad smile on his face.

As the referee ordered the players to return to the field of play, Nathan ran over to where the Hopkins family were sat. He indicated with his forefinger that the goal was for them then returned to his defensive post, barking at the rest of the team to defend as if their lives depended on it for the last quarter of an hour.

After what felt like the longest fifteen minutes of his life, the whistle finally went. Nathan sunk to his knees. It wasn't winning the Community Shield so much - it was not considered a major trophy by any stretch of the imagination - it was what it meant to the club, and particularly the family and friends of Carey Hopkins. There was also the small matter of a challenge he had set himself prior to the final.

Nathan found tears welling up in his eyes as Rideout slapped him on the bag with his giant goalie gloves and gave him a bear hug.

"Well done, mate," the City captain smiled graciously, shaking Nathan's hand. Players from both teams exchanged greetings and milled around in the August sunshine as the sponsors set about erecting the temporary stage in the centre of the pitch.

Nathan's wrist began to ache from shaking hands with so many people, but he wasn't complaining. The BBC and Sky were desperately trying to secure an interview with him, but he dodged their ?? wanting to savour his moment in the sun with his teammates first of all.

"Fantastic header," Brooksy commented, standing a few feet away from Nathan, nervous about approaching him after over a week of no contact with the club captain.

"Thank you, Brooksy," Nathan nodded, smiling. He paused briefly before stepping forward and embracing the shorter man.

Thank fuck for that, Brooksy thought, relieved, returning the bear hug from a hot and sweat-drenched Nathan. The tension, from his side, had been unbearable.

"You better go," Brooksy nodded towards Ziegler, who was gathering the team into a line-up behind the runners-up.

The usual formalities took place, with thanks dutifully

paid to the sponsors and the officials, with a poignant nod to the extremely difficult circumstances in which the match had taken place.

Nathan clapped politely as one by one, the City players received their runners up medals, with the majority neglecting to put the silverware around their necks, a gesture Nathan could understand, even if it did feel somewhat ungracious.

Finally it was Rangers' turn. The boss went first, followed by Ziegler. Mackay, as vice captain, led the players to collect their medals. As Sky Sports Man of the Match, Nathan had been instructed to bring up the rear, to receive his individual trophy before raising the giant octagonal silver trophy aloft.

He handed the MVP award to Brooksy in the backrow as he prepared to raise the trophy with his teammates. Brooksy ran his fingers over the engraved Nathan Hunt Man of the Match then stared at the no.6 shirt in front of him.

With a slapping of the thighs and a crescendoing *Waaahhhhh*, the stadium announcer finally declared North West Rangers the worthy winners of this year's Community Shield. Fireworks exploded as Nathan and Tango held the unwieldy trophy aloft.

The crowd roared along to the obligatory *We are the Champions* before descending into a medley of their favourite songs, from *He's a Cunt* in honour of Nathan's match-winning performance, to the altogether tamer *Shirts of Red, Shorts of Blue, North West Rangers, We love you!*

25

Leaving his young teammates to buffoon around on the makeshift stage, Nathan allowed himself to be led over to the Perspex sponsors wall, where several well-known sports journos were eagerly stood with microphones. Nathan was handed a giant mike with the SkySports logo on it.

"Nathan Hunt, Captain Marvel and Man of the Match, how does it feel?"

"Bloody fantastic!" Nathan laughed, despite the nervous anxiety of what he was about to say.

"How does it feel to score the winning goal in a cup final?"

"Painful!" Nathan grinned, clutching his head.

"You really smacked it one, didn't you?" the female presented laughed.

"Yeah, leathered it. I think I took out a lot of frustration on that ball," Nathan acknowledged more soberly.

"It has been an incredibly difficult time for the club. The manager said in the media conference yesterday that you all wanted to win this in memory of Carey Hopkins."

Nathan nodded, turning serious. "What happened to Carey was terrible and our sympathies go to his family, who are with us today. Jason, Susie and George - this one's for you." He stuck his thumb up towards them in the distant stand and a thousand cameras panned to capture their reaction for the online and paper copies.

Brooksy liked the way he didn't patronise the younger brother of Carey, but rather treated him as an adult along with the parents. Nathan really was a very thoughtful guy, despite his tendency to be taciturn. When he did speak, it was worth it, Brooksy thought.

"What does it mean to be voted Most Valuable Player today?"

Nathan shook his head firmly. Holding the microphone tightly, he looked out to the eighty odd thousand Mancunians packed into Wembley stadium. "Today is not about my performance or anyone else's for that matter. Today is about what happened to Carey and for all the young guys out there struggling with their mental health."

The crowd fell silent. Nathan felt his heart thumping beneath his sweat-drenched wet red shirt.

"I have permission from Carey's parents, the Club's owners, and from the police, to speak out today."

You could have heard a pin drop. Brooksy stood in Nathan's line of vision, several yards away, alongside Lucia and others on the fringes of the team celebration. But Nathan wasn't looking at Brooksy, but at his own perspiring face magnified on the giant screen. He wiped the moisture from his eyes and his beard. This was it. This was his life changing moment.

Brooksy held his breath, sensing a reveal of some sort. But he could never have expected what followed.

"Carey Hopkins killed himself because he was being teased by his teammates."

A gentle rumble of disapproval rippled through the spectators.

"Not because he was ginger, or skinny or freckled, though they teased him about that as well," Nathan paused." Nathan paused. "He killed himself because he was teased for being gay."

The crowd fell silent again. Here goes…. Nathan said to himself.

"As a gay man myself, like Carey, I abhor what happened to him."

Nathan saw eighty thousand mouths open wide, including Brooksy's. Cameras began to furiously click at this game-changing, nay, history-changing statement.

Nathan heard his own voice echo around the giant stadium as he continued.

"Nobody in the 21st century should be made to feel ashamed for being gay. Carey was a fantastic footballer, but he was also a son, a brother and - a man."

The applause began slowly then crescendo-ed into a deafening sound. Nathan stood resolute and proud, eyes now dry. Brooksy felt his heart beating wildly, overflowing
with love and pride for this life-changing statement Nathan had just made - a life-changer for thousands upon thousands of gay boys and men the world over - not just for him and all those associated with Carey Hopkins.

Nathan just stood there, shaking his head, as the crowd, City fans included, broke into an impromptu chant of He hates cunt, He hates cunt, he's Nathan Hunt.

"I guess that bit will be edited for TV," Nathan laughed to the female reporter next to him, but his voice was drowned out by the wall of noise.

He suddenly felt a tap on his arm. He turned to see Jason Hopkins next to him, supported by a Wembley steward. The man was in tears. Nathan took him in his arms and hugged him as tightly as was humanly possible as the older man sobbed uncontrollably. The crowd gradually quietened again.

"I want to speak," Jason told the reporter, voice cracked. She looked at Nathan, who nodded. Nathan held the mike in front of Jason, who appeared barely able to stand.

Nathan appealed for silence and got it. The crowd would have died for him at that precise moment in time.

"My name's Jason, and I'm Carey's dad," Jason Hopkins announced in a broad Manchester accent.

"Nathan is right. Our Carey was gay. But I don't want his teammates to get the blame for what happened to our lad. I am just as guilty if not more, as Carey's dad. I'm ashamed to say…" he started sobbing. "Just give me a moment," he sniffed, as Nathan continued to hold the huge mike in front of him.

"I'm ashamed to say that I rejected him, too. If anyone's to blame, it's me. I was his dad, and I told him I couldn't accept him as he was. I'll have to live with that for the rest of my days. So if you're a father or a parent of a gay son or daughter, please, please, don't do what I did."

He broke down and handing the mike back, Nathan wrapped the man against his giant frame, squeezing his eyes tightly shut to fight back his own tears this time.

At that point, Owen French and Juan-Pedro Morales stepped up to the microphone.

"We would just like to read a statement from the club," Morales began.

"North West Rangers does not condone any form of

discrimination, and that includes homophobia, biphobia or transphobia. We are all collectively guilty at this club of not calling out homophobia. And that starts in the dressing room with the very youngest players, all the way up to the first team. Anyone, ourselves included, who makes any comment that seeks to hurt or intimidate a player or staff member on account of their sexuality, will be banned for life from this club. That includes verbal or non-verbal gestures, as well as physical intimidation. But more than that, we issue an open invitation to any local football players who are LBGT- whatever your age - ”

Nathan forgave him in the circumstances for getting the letters the wrong way around.

“- to come and train with us at a new open training session to be held on Friday evenings, which will be attended by a mixture of youth team and first team players. We hope to have different age group sessions. Who knows, if you’re any good, we might even give you a contract!”

There was laughter.

“Furthermore,” Morales continued, taking the carefully prepared statement from French. “We will be bringing out a new training shirt. It will be purple, Carey’s favourite colour, with Carey’s name across the middle. We will be donating all proceeds from the sale of this shirt to two local charities which support male mental health and LGBT youth. Nathan - if you would do us the honours…”

Morales produced a large purple shirt from a carrier bag.

“I could do with a change of shirt,” Nathan laughed,

removing his shirt to the catcalls of the spectators. He pulled the purple training top over his head, which had Carey Hopkins emblazoned across the front with the strapline "always in our hearts" below. On the back was the number 17, Hopkins' youth team squad number, and his name. Nathan did a twirl for the camera, then arms aloft, started clapping. Eighty thousand spectators joined in and Carey's picture was put up the giant screens once more.

He left the pitch and aimed for the tunnel to the soundtrack of *He hates cunt, he hates cunt... he's Nathan Hunt!*

Life would never be the same again.

NOT THE END

Useful telephone numbers

Samaritans

116 123 (free call any time)

Switchboard LGBT+ helpline

0300 330 060 (10am – 10pm)

About the author

Carol A Shepherd is an author, college lecturer and LGBT faith activist from Eastleigh, near Southampton, UK. You can find her books at www.carolshepherdbooks.info

If you valued this book, the author would greatly appreciate a review to spread the word.

You can also subscribe to Carol's newsletter, The Bi Christian Writer
https://www.subscribepage.com/bichristianwriter

More titles from Easy Yoke Publishing can be found at www.easyyoke.org